Thorne sighed again. He didn't like Field being the chief suspect. This was because he had, almost at once, felt a sense of affinity with the banker. He and Field were alike in many ways. They were both about the same age, both of working-class origin and both intensely ambitious. Thorne disliked being the agent of the other's ruin.

'What we need to know,' he said, 'is how long the poison had been in that flask.'

By the same author

Vac
I Hear Voices
Tornado Pratt

PAUL ABLEMAN

A Killing on the Exchange

GRAFTON BOOKS
A Division of the Collins Publishing Group

LONDON GLASGOW
TORONTO SYDNEY AUCKLAND

Grafton Books
A Division of the Collins Publishing Group
8 Grafton Street, London W1X 3LA

A Grafton Paperback Original 1987

ISBN 0-586-07328-0

Printed and bound in Great Britain by
Collins, Glasgow

Set in Times

1

Superintendent Thorne sat at his desk in his office on the fourth floor of Wood Street Police Station in the City of London writing his concluding report on the Woodvine case. The report stated that Albert Woodvine, head of the accountancy firm, Rook and Raglan, had fallen accidentally from the catwalk across the atrium of the new Eastern Standard Bank building. The report would, Thorne knew, be received sceptically by his superiors but it would ultimately be accepted. The scepticism would be because all the evidence suggested that Woodvine had either been murdered or had committed suicide.

The accountant had been embezzling money for the last five years and stashing it away in various tax refuges around the world. He had thus far appropriated something like three and a half million pounds, a substantial sum if not overwhelming by the standards of present-day City fraud. There was also evidence to suggest that he might have been in the bad books of a notorious gangland figure. But perhaps even more suggestive of unnatural death was the fact that the three-storey-high catwalk from which Woodvine had fallen had been specifically designed to thwart both accidents and all but the most determined suicides. Nevertheless Thorne had patiently assembled enough evidence to convince, he felt, any objective reader that the fall had in fact been accidental.

It gave Superintendent Thorne no pleasure to submit a report of accidental death. There was no glory in it.

What Thorne liked was a difficult homicide cleverly solved. Thorne was ambitious. He was very ambitious indeed.

He was in the middle of dictating the final sentence of the report into his micro-recorder when his private phone rang. He ignored the electronic bleep for a moment or two while he finished speaking the sentence. Then he clicked off the little machine and picked up the receiver.

'Yes?' he asked crisply.

'Lance, is that you?' came the voice of his wife, Milly.

She sounded as if she were standing on an Alp in a roaring gale and Thorne realized that she must be at the wheel of her Jaguar and doubtless exceeding the speed limit on a motorway.

'Milly?' he asked sharply. 'Where are you?'

'Just past Oxford, I think,' came back the voice which was charmingly endowed with a discreet American accent.

'And what on earth are you doing at Oxford?' asked Thorne irritably. 'You didn't tell me you were going out this afternoon?'

'But the estate agent phoned about the house,' returned Milly.

Thorne sighed.

'What house?' he asked.

'Oh, Lance,' pleaded Milly. 'You remember that nice estate agent in Bath who said he'd phone if anything suitable came on the market? Well he phoned this afternoon and the place sounds terrific. I felt I should see it straight away. Country cottages go so quickly these days.'

Thorne smiled to himself. Milly's idea of a country cottage was admittedly something less magnificent than

Chatsworth – but not all that much less magnificent. Thorne himself had no desire at all to acquire any property other than their very attractive town house in the Boltons. He was afraid of possessions – or rather he was afraid of the added complications they could introduce into a life he wished to keep relatively simple for the real challenge of police work. This made it rather awkward that his wife was worth a good many million pounds.

It was not that Thorne was ascetic. He appreciated the good things of life. Although he had not, before acquiring his American heiress wife, been able to afford anything very lavish in the way of high living he had easily acquired a taste for good food and wine. He appreciated driving powerful and well-behaved cars. He liked owning a hand-made shotgun for shooting-parties on grand estates. But for someone who intended one day to be, as he sometimes put it humorously to Milly, 'England's top cop', pleasures were also distractions and above all Thorne was jealous of anything that distracted him from his work. It seemed to him obvious that the acquisition of a large country house would prove a king-sized distraction. Nevertheless after months of rearguard argument, he had finally allowed Milly to persuade him that he would be spared any exertion connected with the 'country cottage'. Milly would, she promised, do everything from buying it to furnishing it herself.

He changed the subject.

'How fast are you driving?' he asked suspiciously.

'Slow,' Milly reassured him. 'Under eighty.'

'Liar,' said Thorne amiably. 'I can tell from the engine. You're doing well over a hundred.'

In the driver's seat of the streaking Jaguar, Milly gasped in dismay at this fake detective work. Ever since he had rescued her from those brutes in Corsica, she had been in awe of his powers of detection. In this case, they were pure bluff. Thorne could tell nothing from the sounds reaching him through the radio telephone as to the Jaguar's speed. He had based his accusation solely on a knowledge of his wife's proclivities.

'Gee,' she exclaimed, as she braked hard, 'You're right. It's so easy in this car. You just don't notice how your speed creeps up. Anyway I'm down to seventy now. It's perfectly safe, Lance. There's not another vehicle in sight.'

'Liar,' said Thorne firmly. 'I can hear loads of traffic.'

Milly gasped again. One of the many juggernauts hemming her in swung out into the fast lane and began to trundle past her at far above its legal limit. Lance had made another inspired guess.

'Oh, Lance,' pleaded Milly. 'Don't say things like that.'

'But, Milly,' expostulated Thorne, 'you promised you wouldn't get into any more trouble. Anyway, why did you phone?'

'Well, I was going to cook tonight, remember? Now I won't be able to. Shall we eat out?'

'Alright,' said Thorne. 'I'll see you at home.'

'Love you,' said Milly and switched off her radio phone.

After Thorne had hung up, he sat for a few seconds, looking at the phone and shaking his head ruefully. He had just decided to ring Milly back and say something a little more affectionate when there was a slight tap at his door and Sergeant Ballantyne entered.

Ballantyne was Thorne's chosen assistant. As a superintendent Thorne rated an inspector as right-hand man but when Ballantyne had joined the City force, a few months previously, Thorne had been sufficiently impressed by his record to have made successful efforts to secure his services.

Ballantyne was, in fact, almost Thorne's opposite in terms of background, temperament and education. Where Thorne was of working-class origins, Ballantyne was a product of a Scottish middle-class family. The young sergeant's father had been a consultant at the Royal Infirmary of Edinburgh. Thorne had begun his career as a village bobby and then, by dint of hard work and much reading, had lifted himself to his present position which was that of the youngest superintendent in the City force and one of the youngest in England. Ballantyne had a degree in PPE from Cambridge. In spite of the differences between the two men, however, there was also an easy sympathy. Both were free of class-consciousness and both of them had a sense of humour.

'What's up?' asked Thorne as the tall young Scot entered his office.

'Call, sir,' said Ballantyne. 'You were on your private line and so it was switched through to me. A banker has been found dead in a sealed office. The security staff at the bank had to break the door down to get in.'

Thorne frowned slightly.

'Any reason to think it wasn't a heart attack?'

'Well, the firm's doctor won't sign the death certificate,' elaborated Ballantyne. 'He wants an autopsy.'

'Which bank?' asked Thorne.

'It's called Carr Sillmann,' replied Ballantyne. 'I think it's a merchant bank.'

'It is,' confirmed Thorne. 'One of the best.'

Carr Sillmann was, Thorne knew, a member of the

9

élite accepting houses committee. It was one of the very few merchant banks whose promissory notes had almost the status of currency. Such institutions were the interface between the world of finance and that of industry. They were greyhound institutions, unlike the giant clearing banks which basically operated by keeping a small percentage of the vast torrents of money that poured through their nets. The merchant banks went out and worked in the world, performing functions like advising foreign governments on how to make the best of their national resources or fighting takeover battles between big corporations at home.

It was the merchant banks which, in the nineteenth century, had funded the projects which had transformed the planet. Canals, railroads, steamships and finally airlines had all in their day been funded by the merchant banks. Thorne remembered reading somewhere that even if the steam engine had been invented in the seventeenth century, railways could not have been built then because there would have been no way to finance them. But the merchant banks kept pace with science and technology. In the nineteenth century they had raised the capital to build the Suez Canal and the Trans-Siberian railway and now the most far-sighted of them were drawing up plans for spaceships and industrial production on the moon.

'Right,' continued Thorne. 'You'd better get the car. I'll be with you in five minutes.'

He devoted some of the five minutes to calling Milly back. She was now winding along a country road at a docile sixty miles an hour. Thorne apologized for his earlier gruffness. Milly was delighted to hear from him again so soon and said the countryside was superb and she had great hopes of the house.

2

Lancelot Thorne was a Cornishman. He had been
brought up in a small seaside hotel in Penzance. Lance
had been only five when his father, a dairy farmer,
had died. His mother, somewhat higher in the social
scale than his father, had been a schoolteacher when
his parents had met. She had given up her career to
help on the farm and raise Lance but after her husband's death had decided that she did not want to go
on running the farm alone. She had sold it and used
the proceeds to buy a small house on the sea front.
She had converted it into a comfortable bed-and-
breakfast establishment and, over the years, had built
on annexes and extensions until she had proudly felt
entitled to advertise it as a hotel.

Lance was her only child. She had begun to suspect
that he was remarkable while he was still only a boy.
He had combined hardiness and athleticism with a
powerful impulse to learn. He could ride and shoot
well while still only just in his teens and he was one of
the best swimmers at the local comprehensive. With
his natural talents he could easily have gone on to
university but he had decided against it. He wanted to
be a policeman.

He had developed this ambition after reading the
memoirs of Sir Martin Gaines. Sir Martin had risen
from being a bobby on the beat to commissioner of
the Metropolitan police and Lance had decided that
he would do the same. He was quite serious about it
and when teachers or his mother pointed out that he

would have to display talents superior to those of several hundred thousand other policemen he proclaimed that he intended to do just that. Basing himself on the example of Sir Martin he decided that the way to the top in the police service starts at the bottom. At the age of eighteen, therefore, he had joined the police and, after training, had spent the next three years as a village bobby.

Thorne spoke with a faint Cornish accent. He could, he knew, quite easily have shed the accent if he had wanted. But he preferred to keep his origins in the forefront of his life. He was a man who liked to keep things out in the open.

Thorne had joined the City of London force five years previously. He had been posted from Bristol with the rank of inspector. In Bristol he had been number two in the regional CID. When he had reached the City he had set himself to learn as much as he could about his new posting. This meant, for Thorne, not only familiarizing himself with the special forms of crime, such as fraud, bullion robbery, counterfeiting and so forth, which are indigenous to a great financial centre but also with the historical background of the area.

He read books on the origins of banking. He learned, for example, that Lombard Street was so called in honour of the Italians who had invented modern banking in the fifteenth century. Amongst many other things he had learned how the merchant banks had arisen. The earliest merchant bankers, in the eighteenth century, had been merchants whose name had been a byword for honesty and whose promissory notes had therefore acquired the status of currency. By degrees these merchants had found it more profitable to trade in integrity rather than in wool, cotton or other commodities. By the mid-nineteenth century modern merchant banking had been established.

In the car on the way to the offices of Carr Sillmann, Thorne explained some of these things to Ballantyne. The sergeant had also done a certain amount of background reading but he had only been with the City force for a few months. Surprisingly, considering his university education, he was not as quick a scholar as Thorne who had always shown a talent for grasping the essentials of a subject. When Thorne and Ballantyne were alone there was usually a great deal of talk between them which often took the form of Thorne instructing Ballantyne in some aspect of police work. But when the two plain-clothes detectives were with the public Ballantyne usually became a silent and respectful background presence.

Thorne had never before entered the premises of Carr Sillmann. But he had often passed its discreet façade in small street just off Grocers' Walk. The merchant banks were not gaudy institutions. They did not go in for skyscraper buildings with towering entrance halls that might contain miniature jungles, running streams and even waterfalls. They did not need to impress anyone. The merchant banks did not solicit custom from the public at large but only from industrialists and businessmen. For such professionals reputation was what counted while ostentation was suspect.

Although his duties had never before taken him to Carr Sillmann, Thorne had been in a number of other top merchant banks. He knew the twin characteristics common to all of them. They were always part fortresses and part luxury hotels. They all had large security staffs. Sensitive areas were protected by television scanners, electronic locks and complex alarm systems. Checks were kept on anyone entering or leaving. But the merchant banks also boasted opulent drawing rooms and dining rooms, equipped with splendid furniture, fine silver and the best food and wines. There were butlers and other servants to cater for senior staff and especially for clients. It was the Rothschild bank which, in the nineteenth century, had institutionalized the lunch as a key weapon in merchant banking. Monarchs and international financiers had, over the gastronomic splendours of a Rothschild lunch, devised schemes for linking oceans with canals and stitching together continents with iron rails.

Carr Sillmann had been founded in the thirties by Sir Max Sillmann. He had not then, of course, been a knight. Although part-Jewish and originally from Berlin he had nevertheless not come to England in the early thirties as a refugee from Nazism. He had come to learn two things: English and merchant banking and he had mastered both. By the mid-eighties his organization was considered the best merchant bank in the City of London.

Thorne and Ballantyne were greeted in the foyer by Carr Sillmann's chief security officer, a wiry, anxious-looking man called Jack Candlepayne. As Candlepayne led them through the corridors and up in the lift to the dead man's office he told them what he knew. It seemed the victim was one Charles Makepeace, who had been head of corporate finance. Thorne knew enough about modern merchant banking to understand that the corporate finance department is usually the senior branch of a merchant bank. It is responsible for buying and selling companies on behalf of its clients and also for raising capital for purposes like business

14

expansion. But, in recent years, the most newsworthy and influential activity of a corporate finance department has undoubtedly been conducting takeover bids.

As headlines have testified, a kind of takeover fever has recently gripped the world's financial centres. A lot of this activity stems from the impulse, as old as capitalism, to acquire a monopoly. If you control all the means of producing a particular product you can, in theory at least, charge as much as you like for it. But nowadays most modern countries put limits on the growth of monopolies. So takeover fever does not stem exclusively from the monopoly instinct. Greater efficiency, more power, increased profits are some of the many reasons why takeovers are attempted. And then, unlike most commercial activities, a takeover battle appeals to the sporting instinct. It is somewhat like a team sport and the best side, usually meaning the side which retains the best merchant bank, often wins.

Candlepayne told them discreetly that Charles Makepeace had been a heavy drinker and a man with a sharp tongue which had made him disliked by many of his colleagues. He had also been feared because of his influence on the head of the firm, Sir Max, whose oldest colleague he had been.

When Candlepayne had finished divulging this information, Thorne thanked him and then said:

'I gather you had to break the door down, Jack?'

'That's right,' admitted Candlepayne.

'Why was that?' asked Thorne.

'It had a combination lock.'

'So I'd have thought,' acknowledged Thorne. 'But why didn't you just open it with the combination?'

Candlepayne smiled, a trifle sheepishly.

'The thing is, superintendent, only two people know

the combinations to these locks. One is the executive who has the office – and he was inside, dead. The other is me – and I couldn't remember it.'

'You couldn't what?' asked Thorne incredulously. 'Well why didn't you look it up? It must be filed somewhere.'

Candlepayne shook his head sadly.

'It's not,' he admitted. 'I've always relied on memory. I mean security's not really security if the thing's written down, is it?'

'You mean – ' Thorne began, trying to digest this extraordinary admission, but Candlepayne interrupted.

'Don't rub it in, superintendent. Needless to say, I remembered the combination just as the door caved in under the axe.'

'Well, they're your doors,' said Thorne mildly. 'I take it you keep a log book? Or do you depend on memory for that too?'

'I've got a log book,' said Candlepayne gruffly as they turned a corner and saw a uniformed constable on guard, looking very incongruous in those surroundings, standing beside the wreck of a door hanging from its hinges.

'I'll need to see it. Now before we arrive, is there anything else you can tell me?'

Candlepayne shook his head.

'I'm a locks and alarms man, superintendent. Homicide's not my line.'

'So you think it's homicide, do you?' asked Thorne sharply.

There was a slight pause and then Candlepayne replied:

'Dr Mellors seems to.'

This did not turn out to be strictly true. Doctor Mellors was waiting for them in Makepeace's office.

He was a pleasant-looking young man with receding gingery hair and an air of competence. When Thorne mentioned homicide to him he immediately protested that he could not tell how Charles Makepeace had died. All he knew was that there were certain medical signs on his body which didn't seem totally compatible with a heart attack.

'What signs?' asked Thorne, watching two policemen making measurements on the floor around a bulky and utterly still man who was stretched out upon it.

It seemed these signs were very subtle: a minor enlargement of certain lymph nodes, a slight discolouration of the finger nails.

'Poison?' asked Thorne.

Mellors said crisply:

'That's obviously one possibility. But the signs don't point to any poison that I know about, superintendent.'

'Thank you,' said Thorne.

With Ballantyne he walked slowly across the sumptuously furnished and quite extensive office to the body. Charles Makepeace lay on his stomach beside a tan leather sofa. On a small table beside the body stood a silver hip flask without an accompanying glass. If Makepeace had drunk anything from that flask, Thorne realized, he must have drunk it directly from the vessel in the traditional way.

Thorne squatted down beside the bulky corpse. Robbed of the sharp tongue he was supposed to have had in life, Makepeace looked plumply endearing. His pink-grained complexion, doubtless testimony to damaged circulation, made him look a bit like a great cuddly toy.

Thorne did not touch the body and after a brief inspection of it stood up again. He instructed Ballantyne to make sure all relevant pathological investigations were carried out. He wanted the full routine for suspected murder: measurements of position, photographs, finger-prints, dust, fibre – anything that might be useful. But most of all he wanted to know two things: what had been inside the hip flask and what was still inside Charles Makepeace. Until such time as he knew these things there was nothing he could usefully do at Carr Sillmann and so he proposed to go back to Wood Street and catch up on some paper-work.

Four hours later Thorne learned what he had expected. A poison had been found both in the flask and in Makepeace's body. It was an industrial poison but one that was contained in so many domestic products that almost anyone could have obtained some.

3

Sir Max leaned back in his tilting, green-leather chair.

'Charles thought England was in decline,' he said.

Sir Max was a tall, hawk-nosed, white-haired man with the kind of bronzed complexion that usually comes from cruises or holidays in places like the Bahamas.

After Sir Max's initial remark he looked at Thorne as if half-expecting a comment. Thorne, however, nodded encouragingly but remained silent. Sir Max resumed.

'Yes, he hated the changes in the class structure, the loss of the Empire, immigration, all the things that have happened since the war. He was a crotchety man. He rubbed people up the wrong way.'

Sir Max, Thorne noted, had scarcely a trace left of his original German accent. His office was large and two-thirds of it resembled a particularly well furnished Regency drawing room rather than a banker's office.

'Made enemies, did he?' asked Thorne.

'Undoubtedly,' nodded Sir Max, 'but not, I should have thought, homicidal ones. He was my oldest colleague, you know. Indeed he was my first employee.'

'What about his domestic life?' asked Thorne.

'Oh, extremely happy,' said Sir Max with no hesitation. 'His wife is a delightful lady who was once successful in business herself. Has it been definitely ascertained that Mr Makepeace didn't die of natural causes?'

Thorne nodded.

'He was poisoned.'

'Painful?' asked Sir Max.

'Variable,' said Thorne. 'This particular poison would have produced about the same effect as a heart attack.'

'I assumed that's what it was – a heart attack – when I first heard. And it didn't surprise me. He was a sick man, you know?'

'How sick?'

'Well his heart was in poor condition. He drank rather a lot – '

'In spite of his happy marriage?'

'Well – pressure. The City's a killer to senior executives, superintendent. There was no difficulty with his marriage, as I've said. You won't find any scandal associated with Charles.' Sir Max glanced at his watch. Thorne noted the glance. He had long ago observed that people glance at their watches when they don't like the course of a conversation. 'Is there anything else I can tell you, superintendent?'

Thorne said quickly:

'Yes, sir. Everything.'

An astonished look appeared on Sir Max's face. There was not, it seemed to Thorne, any anxiety mixed in with it.

'I beg your pardon?' asked the head of Carr Sillmann.

Thorne smiled.

'Oh, I realize you're much too busy, sir' Thorne quickly went on. 'But I wonder if you could lend me one of your employees – someone who knows pretty much everything that's been happening in Mr Makepeace's department?'

Sir Max smiled.

'You're an information man, are you, superintendent? Good. I like that. Very well – I'll think of someone. John Field would probably be best – although he's going to be very busy. He'll be taking over corporate finance, Charles's department. At a very difficult moment, I may say. We're on the edge of a big takeover battle.'

'Really?' asked Thorne with a faintly 'raised eyebrows' look.

Sir Max shook his head.

'Oh no, superintendent. Takeovers can be pretty rough these days. Plenty of dirty tricks – but not murder! Tell you what, I'll phone down now and see if John can see you.'

When the call from his boss reached him John Field was in fact reading the third of five reports that he had to master before lunching with a client. Of course he did not read every word of each of them. They averaged about fifteen thousand words long. John had never actually learned speed reading but he had perforce become quite good at it. He found he could run his eyes quickly down a page and absorb the vital information, and especially the figures, that it contained. It was a talent many merchant bankers acquired for without it, even with the help of computers, it would have been difficult, if not impossible, to assimilate the huge quantities of information needed to make daily decisions involving millions of pounds.

John only had about half an hour left in which to finish reading the reports when his intercom buzzed and his secretary told him that Sir Max would like a word with him. After he had listened to Sir Max's request, and hung up the phone again, he did not resume his reading. Instead he sat back in his chair with a troubled expression. It seemed that a superintendent of police was on his way over to question him and the fact was that John Field was very reluctant to tell him the truth – or at least the whole truth.

He knew by now, as did most of the senior staff at Carr Sillmann, that Charles Makepeace had probably been murdered. He also knew that he himself could not help being high on the list of suspects. After all, he had been number two to Charles in corporate finance, and the heir apparent is always a suspect should the king be killed. In this case suspicion would be increased by the well-known fact that there had been animosity between Charles and him. John Field smiled grimly. It hadn't been of an adult nature, that animosity. More like the sort of thing that happens on a school playground, the result of teasing and bullying. For John Field was a man of humble origins and Charles Makepeace had never let him forgt it.

John's mind went back to their last meeting. This, now that he considered it, had occurred the night before – on the very evening before Charles's nocturnal death. Conceivably John had been the last person to talk to Makepeace.

John had been returning from making a routine inquiry in the dealing room. As he passed the half-opened door to Charles's office, Charles had called out:

'John, could I have a word with you?'

John had, of course, immediately responded by poking his head around the door. Charles had smiled broadly and said with apparent enthusiasm:

'Good news, you'll have some help with the Dinslow takeover.'

John was wary of Charles's apparent cordiality. He asked doubtfully:

22

'Are you saying that I'll be in charge?'

Charles nodded. 'For the first and last time, I shouldn't wonder. Come in, come in. Yes, you'll have your future boss to help you.'

John entered and approached Charles's desk.

'My what?' he asked.

Charles smiled again but this time with a hint of open malice.

'Daniel Maitland.'

'The American? But he's not due for another month.'

'Been put forward.'

John frowned.

'But why do you call him my future boss, Charles?'

The other gestured expansively. 'Oh, not immediately, of course. But when I retire.'

John usually let Charles's gibes pass unchallenged but this one was too important to be ignored.

'Charles,' he said firmly. 'I'm number two in corporate finance.'

Charles chuckled faintly.

'You're priceless, John. Dan Maitland's father owns one of the ten biggest banks in America. Now I believe you went to a comprehensive in the East End, didn't you?'

John was used to this sort of mockery. It was true. He was a Cockney. His father owned a corner shop in the East End. John had worked hard to become an accountant and finally a merchant banker. He was neither ashamed of his origins nor of his family. But he did get a little bored sometimes with Charles Makepeace's endless jeering.

'I'm still number two in this department, Charles,' he insisted.

Charles nodded.

'But I doubt if you will be for long after Maitland gets here, old boy. Sir Max knows how important breeding is in merchant banking. Now when I first came to the City, you'd have been lucky to get a job as an office boy.'

John contemplated him silently. He knew perfectly well that Charles was bluffing. For several years now John had done all the hard work, and made the difficult decisions, in the department. He also suspected that Sir Max knew this. And yet it was just possible that Charles, who was an old comrade of Sir Max's, might still be able to block his promotion.

That particular exchange had, John was pretty sure, been private. It was conceivable that Nina, Charles's secretary, could have caught some of it when she had briefly appeared in the office with a message, or could have heard something on the internal intercom. But far more important, as regards John's present anxiety about the police, was the fact that Nina would certainly tell the police that she had heard similar angry exchanges between him and Charles in the past.

John was not, of course, seriously worried that his strained relations with his superior might ultimately lead him to the dock. He was much more concerned that they might provoke investigations by the police which would lead to them discovering *his* secret. Which brought him, as he went on brooding on the events of the evening before, to his meeting at Fenchurch Street station.

On time for once, John had left Carr Sillmann at about five-thirty and had made his way to the station. He shouldn't really have left that early. As always there were many things he should have done before leaving the building. But on that particular evening he had to leave on time. He had an appointment with Kate MacRenny, his mistress.

Kate was a stockbroker of Irish descent. She was twenty-six years old, red-haired and most attractive. She and John had met at a City thank-you party two and a half years before and had, a little drunkenly, become lovers that same night. The party had gone on until after four in the morning and by chance they had both chosen to spend the remnant of the night in the same hotel where they had met again at the reception desk. They had gone up in the lift together and then, almost without a word being exchanged, they had entered Kate's bedroom and fallen on to the bed together.

Nevertheless it had occurred to neither of them that it was anything more than a one-night stand. And it would almost certainly not have been more except for the fact that, some two weeks later, they had met, again quite by chance, in a queue at a butcher's shop in Leadenhall Market and, after nervous smiles and greetings, had wound up deep in conversation. They had then realized that they were not just compatible physically, as they had discovered after the thank-you party, but that they enjoyed talking and laughing together. Kate, unlike John's wife, could share City gossip with him and she also had the same sense of the absurd. They had made a date for lunch the next day. They had both, very riskily and unethically, taken the afternoon off to go back to Kate's place to make love, and thereafter they had seen as much of each other as they could manage for the next two and a half years.

'John Field, isn't it?' asked Kate ironically, tapping him on the shoulder from behind.

He turned abruptly with a smile but before he could say anything she continued:

'I recognized you straight away. That's pretty good, don't you think, considering how long it's been?'

John looked penitent.

'I know – and I'm sorry. I've missed you.'

Kate said petulantly:

'Well, I wish you wouldn't. You tell me I'm free. And just when I'm getting used to the idea you chase after me.'

'Look, Kate,' said John, glancing around circumspectly before stooping and giving her a quick kiss on the lips. 'We've got a takeover coming up. I'll be spending nights in town again.'

'Will you now?' asked Kate. 'And who's taking over whom?'

'John grinned and, in an exaggerated Cockney accent, said:

'What you after then, girl? They lock you up for collusion, you know?'

One of the things that convinced John that he and Kate had a real relationship was the fact that she was the only person in the world with whom he was unselfconscious about his Cockney origins. He could no more have put on a Cockney accent with his wife, or with any of his colleagues, than he could have slapped Sir Max on the back. But with Kate he felt completely at ease.

He reverted to his normal accent.

'We could see a lot of each other, Kate,' he said eagerly.

'Lucky old me,' replied the girl reflectively, 'but the fact is, John Field, I'm wondering if I'm really cut out to be an independent woman. And I do hate deceiving your wife. So don't be surprised if one day you snap your fingers and no one comes running. Meanwhile, it will be nice to see more of you.'

Thinking back on the meeting, John shivered slightly with alarm at the thought of the police finding out about Kate. It would inevitably mean that Grace, his wife, would also learn of her existence. He didn't want to lose Kate, certainly, but even less did he want to hurt his wife. He felt easy and young and completely himself with Kate, while he often felt prematurely middle-aged and somewhat tense with his wife. And yet he had no doubt at all that his marriage was the most important thing in his life.

For one thing, his marriage meant his daughter, Evey, a pretty five-year-old whom he adored. But his feeling for Grace was just as important. Grace's father had been a surgeon and Grace herself, before their marriage, had been a doctor, a paediatrician. She had given up her career to raise their child. She had high standards of conduct and service to the community. She was far from humourless but she lacked the hilarious sense of the ridiculous which John appreciated with Kate. For all that, John loved and needed his wife and knew that she loved and needed him.

It seemed wonderful to him when he could, for once, get home on time or even a little early. This was primarily because it gave him a chance to romp with Evey. Their latest game was for John to construct a mock show-jumping course on the back lawn out of deck-chairs, croquet mallets and any other objects that might be lying about the garden. Then, with Evey on his back, he would pretend to be a horse and would go bucking and rolling round the course until they ended up sprawled in a heap together on the fragrant lawn.

On that evening, after their romp, Evey surprised him by asking if she could have a real pony. They could afford it, John knew, but would Grace approve? When he put it to her she vetoed it totally. She had, she said, treated many children who had been in riding accidents and she knew how nasty the results could be. John did not argue.

When Grace got up from the table to get his baked apple, he got his pocket calculator out as inconspicuously as he could and began working out certain profit margins connected with the forthcoming takeover battle. Grace glanced over at him and said irritably:

'What do you think you're doing?'

He replied mildly:

'Just checking a few figures.'

Grace returned peevishly, 'Well, I wish you wouldn't at table. It's barbarous. Do all merchant bankers work as hard as you do?'

John sighed and put his pocket calculator away.

'Yes,' he said. 'If they want to go on being merchant bankers. Darling, we've got another takeover coming up.'

She put the apple down in front of him and exclaimed.

'Oh, God, no. The last time I hardly saw you for the whole six weeks. Who is it this time?'

'Our client is Dinslow Chemicals. They want to take over a downstream outfit called Fane and Browning. The two companies overlap in research. Together they would have good chances for expansion.'

'How splendid!' said Grace sarcastically, 'We certainly need expanded chemical outfits.'

'Look, Grace – '

But Grace had remembered something John had told her earlier in the evening.

'What about this American?' she asked anxiously. 'They won't really give him the department, will they? Just because he's got a rich father?'

'No,' said John with more confidence than he felt.

'When Charles goes, I'll be head of corporate finance. Still I'm looking forward to meeting one Maitland.'

'And when's that likely to be?'

'Tomorrow morning,' said John. He consulted his watch. 'As a matter of fact his plane should be landing at Heathrow just about now.'

4

Carr Sillmann's VIP suite was one of the most impressive in the city, a penthouse on top of a twenty-storey building. It provided what many people considered the finest panoramic views of the City and the Thames. In that enormous glass box of a room financiers and industrialists from all over the world had stayed at one time or another. Now it held Daniel Maitland, who had arrived the evening before and been taken there by a Carr Sillmann limousine.

At nine in the morning John knocked on his bedroom door.

'Come in,' came a thick and muffled voice.

John entered. A tall young man, dressed in singlet and underpants, was standing at one of the twenty-foot-long glass walls – they could hardly be called windows – gazing down in admiration.

'Oh – sorry,' exclaimed John apologetically, noticing how the other was dressed.

The man turned, a friendly smile on his face.

'Okay by me,' he said simply and without embarrassment. 'You must be John Field. Where am I – if it's not a dumb question?'

John blinked in surprise.

'Well, this is our VIP suite. Our driver brought you here last night. Don't you remember?'

Dan shook his head apologetically.

''Fraid not. Fact is, I'm a wet-palm flyer. Always get drunk on planes to try to dull the terror. It never works but it wrecks my memory. Anyway this is certainly very fine hospitality.'

'Glad you like it,' said John. 'You've been assigned to our division – corporate finance.'

'And you're in charge?' asked Dan Maitland.

John shook his head emphatically.

'No, Charles Makepeace is the CO.'

Of course, at that time, John had had no idea that 'the CO' was lying dead in his sealed office. He had continued: 'I'm the second in command.'

'And I'm the new office boy, right?' asked Maitland with a smile.

John wondered for a moment if he was fishing for deference but then decided the young American was simply easy-going. He smiled back and said, 'Not with your background.'

'Oh, I know,' continued Maitland, 'Dad's a big-shot banker. But I'm basically just a tennis player.'

John said, 'Yes, I've heard – Davis Cup.'

'Do you play?'

John shrugged.

'I can swing a racket. And it sometimes connects with the ball. But it's not what you'd call playing. Now then, have you had breakfast?'

Maitland shook his head, and said, 'Eggs and bacon? Now that you mention it I could just use a classic English breakfast.'

John pointed.

'That phone – it connects with our catering staff. Order yourself anything you want. I'll leave you now. When you're ready, I know Sir Max would like to welcome you. And then later in the morning we've got a strategy conference.'

'Strategy conference?' repeated Maitland vaguely.

'To prepare for a takeover battle. I'll fill you in later.'

After he left the hospitality suite, John went straight to Carr Sillmann and spent the first part of the morning at his desk preparing points for his talk at the strategy conference. About mid-morning he heard the first rumours of the death of Charles Makepeace.

By the time Thorne and Ballantine reached his office, John had made up his mind what he would do. As a result, he was completely candid with them about his relations with Makepeace. He told the two detectives about the long antagonism between them. He told them exactly how the department worked. He did not conceal the fact that his last meeting with Charles, only the night before, had been a stormy one. He gave them an almost verbatim account of it. He was completely candid about everything – except Kate. He never mentioned her at all and certainly not his meeting with her at Fenchurch Street after he had left the bank.

When he had finished, he felt that he had been convincing. For this reason he experienced a powerful stab of dismay when Thorne looked at him hard and asked: 'Haven't you left something out, sir?'

So they'd found out about Kate after all and his infidelity to Grace would be made public. How bloody awful!

'What do you mean?' he asked instinctively.

'Why did you come back to the bank about half an hour after you'd left?' asked Thorne.

For a moment John gaped at him, conscious chiefly of a deep feeling of relief.

'What on earth do you – ' he started to expostulate.

And then he remembered. The superintendent was right. John had completely forgotten. After leaving

Kate he'd been hurrying to catch his train when he'd suddenly remembered the Grue-Hartmann file which he needed to study for the next day's strategy conference. He had hurried out of the station, caught a taxi for the short ride back to the bank, gone in and – yes, of course, the security men would have picked him up on their monitor screens as he collected the file and by now the police would know all about it.

He sighed and smiled ruefully at the two detectives.

'I came back for a file,' he explained. 'Actually I'd completely forgotten.'

'Is that all?' asked Thorne lightly. 'Just a file?'

John felt a small tremor of dismay and this time, he knew, it was not about Kate. They couldn't seriously suppose that he had come back to poison Charles Makepeace, could they?

'Yes, that's all – just a file,' he said.

'Right. Thank you, Mr Field,' said Superintendent Thorne pleasantly.

He nodded at his sergeant and then the two policemen rose, said a civil good-bye to the young acting head of corporate finance and departed.

Thorne and Ballantyne had now completed the first stage of their investigation. An hour or so later, as they were collating their information back in Thorne's office, Ballantyne asked:

'Could it have been suicide, sir?'

'Well, it's an elaborate way to top yourself,' said Thorne. 'But technically it could have been suicide. I reckon the odds are about a thousand to one against but we can't eliminate the possibility until we prove that it was murder. And it was murder, sergeant.'

'I suppose Field has to be the chief suspect, doesn't he, sir?' asked Ballantyne.

Thorne sighed. By the book Ballantyne was right.

Field had to be the chief suspect. It was known that he had been on poor terms with his boss. He had a motive: the desire to be head of the department and put a stop to Makepeace's jeering. He had lied to them. He could have returned to the bank on the night of the murder in order to put the poison into Makepeace's flask and might have dodged the surveillance cameras long enough to do it. But in spite of all these suggestive factors Thorne was convinced that Field was innocent. His 'copper's instinct' told him this and Thorne put more trust in that than in the reports of pathological laboratories.

Once, to pass the time on a long train journey, Thorne had tried to analyze what this instinct really was. He had decided that it must be a kind of endless sifting of evidence by his unconscious mind which gave better results than deliberate sifting by his conscious mind. Thorne was convinced that Field was not the murderer because this unconscious sifting told him that John Field could not have poisoned anyone. Oh, Field would have been capable, as almost all human beings are capable, of killing another in a moment of rage, but poison – ? The use of poison argues cold deliberation and lethal planning of a kind that, Thorne was sure, were alien to Field's psychology.

Thorne sighed again. He didn't like Field being the chief suspect. This was because he had, almost at once, felt a sense of affinity with the banker. He and Field were alike in many ways. They were about the same age, both of working-class origin and both intensely ambitious. Thorne disliked the possibility of being the agent of the other's ruin.

'What we need to know,' he said, 'is how long the poison had been in that flask.'

'According to the lab reports,' Ballantyne reminded

him, 'it was stable in alcoholic solution. Could have been there for years.'

'But not,' suggested Thorne with a slight emphasis, 'in the pocket of an alcoholic, eh?'

After a moment he continued:

'So? Who put the poison in the flask?'

Ballantyne said:

'It's obvious who'd have had the best opportunity.'

Thorne grinned.

'You mean his girl friend?'

Ballantyne looked surprised.

'I meant his wife,' he urged. 'Did he have a girl friend?'

'Sir Max was very fierce in defence of his honour – a little too fierce, it struck me. So let's go and interview the ladies, shall we, sergeant?'

'But we don't know who the girl friend was, do we, sir?' objected the mystified sergeant.

'True. But the wife will. They always do.'

Less than half an hour later the two were driving up into one of the most attractive parts of London: the heights of Hampstead. There, in a small, tree-lined square, they ultimately located a delightful cottage which looked exactly as it must have done when completed in the mid-seventeenth century. Its front windows commanded a view of the whole of central and South London and beyond its surrounding brick wall was a large cottage garden.

They entered the eight-foot-high front gate, and Thorne noted that it held a good modern security lock unbolted at present. They went up a short front path to a low flight of steps in front of the door. They rang the bell. It was answered by a thin, elegant lady with, they soon discovered, a touch of ironic wit in her manner. This was Isobel Makepeace, the dead man's widow. Thorne knew from his talk with Sir Max that she was the daughter of a Manchester solicitor and that she had once been a successful businesswoman in her own right.

She offered them tea and Thorne, to Ballantyne's surprise, accepted. Thorne did so because he knew that, in an English context, a cup of tea often unlocks tongues. It seemed to work with Isobel Makepeace. She talked at length and frankly about her relationship with her husband, not disguising the fact that it had become rather bleak in recent years. She did not pretend to be grief-stricken. Indeed at one point she said:

'It seems so gratuitous.'

'What does?' asked Thorne quickly.

'Poisoning Charles,' she specified. 'After all, with his heart he wouldn't have lived long in any case.'

Thorne and Ballantyne exchanged a glance. Thorne said tactfully.

'We've only just established ourselves that your husband was poisoned, Mrs Makepeace. May I ask how you knew?'

She did not seem in the least perturbed.

'From Max – Sir Max Sillmann. He's an old friend. I spoke to him on the phone this morning. He seemed to think Charles had been poisoned. It's true, isn't it?'

Thorne nodded soberly.

'Can you think who might have done it?'

Isobel Makepeace shook her head.

'No, but I know how and when it was done.'

Ballantyne could not restrain himself from uttering a small, surprised gasp at this astonishing claim.

'Go on,' said Thorne encouragingly.

'Well, it must have been last Tuesday week,' said Mrs Makepeace briskly. 'Charles and I were going out to dinner. But when we got to the restaurant, Charles said he was simply too tired to enjoy it and so we came home again. That would have been about nine or quarter past. The very moment we got into the house I knew there was someone else in it.'

'How?' asked Thorne, not sceptically, but with what sounded like keen professional interest.

Mrs Makepeace smiled and said, 'I've lived here for forty years I can feel what's happening in this house. Naturally I immediately went upstairs. He – '

'He?' picked up Thorne quickly.

'Well, I assume it was a "he", superintendent,' she returned a touch irritably, 'because of the climbing involved in breaking into the house. But I suppose it could have been a "she". Anyway whoever it was must have made off when they heard me coming up the stairs.'

'And how did you know for sure anyone had been there?'

'The window was open and so was the cupboard and all the drawers. Nothing had been taken in spite of the fact that I keep jewellery in one of the drawers. I remember thinking at the time it was almost as if the thief had been looking for something specific. Then today when I heard that Charles had been poisoned I realized that it must have been his hip flask. It was actually in the breast pocket of one of his suits in the wardrobe. I'm right, aren't I, superintendent? The poison was in his hip flask?'

Thorne nodded.

'Who do you think might have put it there?' he asked.

Mrs Makepeace shook her head firmly.

'How should I know? I find it hard to believe that anyone – '

She broke off abruptly.

'Well?'

'Oh alright – someone did occur to me but it's ridiculous.'

'Who occurred to you?'

'Well – since you're bound to find out about her in due course, I'll tell you. It was his mistress. She wanted to marry him but he wouldn't. He'd finished with her actually.'

'And you think she would have been capable of poisoning him?'

'No, I don't. I feel sure it was a man. But she's the only person I can think of who had a strong grudge against Charles. Lots of people found him trying – but you don't murder people because they're awkward, do you, superintendent?'

'In my career,' said Thorne a trifle sententiously, 'I have frequently been astonished at how trivial the motives for murder can be. Now, tell me all about this mistress.'

5

Three quarters of an hour later, Ballantyne pulled up the unmarked Rover outside a large block of flats in Maida Vale. The two officers got out. Thorne contemplated the building for a moment.

'Ornamental iron grilles,' he remarked.

Ballantyne asked: 'Is that significant?'

Thorne grinned. He explained:

'Rich men often lodge their mistresses in large blocks of flats with ornamental iron grilles.'

Ballantyne looked duly impressed.

'Oh? Why is that, sir?' he asked.

'The big block is impersonal and that minimizes the chances of being spotted. The ornamental iron grilles compensate by providing a touch of delicacy and romance.'

'Very impressive, sir,' said Ballantyne dutifully.

They had by this time reached the front door with its row of answerphone buttons. Thorne pressed the one corresponding to the number that Mrs Makepeace had given them. He said dismissively:

'And probably pure drivel. Still it can sometimes be useful, sergeant, to sound more perceptive than you really are.'

A female voice issued from the answerphone's speaker:

'Who is it?'

'Superintendent Thorne – City police. May we come up, Miss Tyson?'

Ballantyne noticed that Thorne then seemed to listen

intently. All he could have heard was silence but there was quite a lot of it before the voice came back.

'I suppose so. But I don't see why a policeman should want to see me.'

The buzzer buzzed and the two detectives entered the block of flats.

The woman who opened the door to them on the third floor, a little later, was pretty and apparently in her mid-thirties. She looked much as Thorne had imagined her, having learned from Isobel Makepeace not only that her name was Stella Tyson but also that she was an actress. She looked from Thorne to Ballantyne and asked:

'Has this got anything to do with Charley?'

'Charley?' asked Thorne quickly.

'Charley Makepeace,' she amplified.

'Yes, I'm afraid it has,' said Thorne.

'Well?' asked Stella Tyson anxiously. She opened the door a little further as if to admit them. Thorne, however, did not budge.

'I'm sorry to have to tell you this,' he said firmly, 'but Mr Makepeace is dead.'

He then looked intently at her. Ballantyne realized he was trying to note even small reactions to his harsh statement.

Stella Tyson gazed back at the detective with little change in her expression beyond a slight narrowing of the eyes. Then she nodded.

'Yes, of course,' she murmured. 'Two policemen wouldn't have called to tell me Charley had caught cold, would they? Alright, come in, gentlemen.'

She stepped back and admitted them to a large and comfortable but rather shabby flat. The hall had a faded oriental carpet on the floor, a glass-fronted cabinet holding china and an ornate umbrella stand amongst its more notable features. Stella led them through it into a large drawing room which, like the hall, was overfurnished but attractive. The walls were decorated with theatrical posters and prints.

'Sit down,' said Stella wearily.

When they had done so, she asked: 'When did Charley die?'

'Last night,' said Thorne.

'And you think he's been murdered, is that it?' asked Stella Tyson.

Thorne replied impersonally, 'We're carrying out routine investigations.'

Once more he watched her intently and this time his scrutiny was rewarded. Ballantyne was shocked to see the change in the young woman's expression. Her chin trembled for a moment and then suddenly Stella Tyson uttered a wail of sorrow and buried her face in her hands. She sat down on the sofa and rocked back and forth, weeping. Thorne and Ballantyne waited uncomfortably. The paroxysm lasted for a minute or two. And then, as abruptly as it had begun, it ended. Stella quite visibly pulled herself together. She wiped her eyes. She sat upright. She looked firmly at Thorne.

'Alright,' she said defiantly. 'What do you want from me?'

'You knew, of course,' said Thorne quietly, 'that Mr Makepeace was married?'

Stella replied immediately:

'Of course I did. That's why I refused to marry him. Anyway until last week.'

Thorne frowned.

'Are you saying that you accepted his proposal last week?'

'Exactly. Charley kept saying he'd get a divorce. He pleaded with me to marry him. Finally I agreed.'

'I see,' said Thorne. 'Did Mr Makepeace – how shall I put it? – contribute to your expenses, Miss Tyson?'

Stella smiled faintly. She knew what Thorne was getting at.

'I'm a successful actress, superintendent,' she said. 'I'm not a kept woman. But Charley loved giving me money and so I accepted small sums from time to time.'

Thorne nodded.

'And what made you change your mind about marriage?'

Stella explained without hesitation.

'I found that I could no longer contemplate losing him. I know that to a lot of people he seemed just an old grouch. But to me he was a very understanding friend. So I finally agreed to marry him – after he got his divorce, naturally.'

'And where did this proposal take place?' asked Thorne.

Stella said, 'In the country. We'd driven out of town for lunch. On the way back we stopped at a lay-by – a local beauty spot which had a famous view. After a time, and sounding pessimistic, Charley once more asked me to marry him. And do you know, superintendent, I think I took myself by surprise when I said, "Alright, Charley, I will". So then we drank a toast to our future and – '

'A toast?' Thorne interrupted quickly. 'How could you do that?'

Stella shrugged.

'Charley always carried a hip flask – silver – which his father had given him. He kept it filled with his favourite whisky. It didn't hold much – just a few sips – but it was enough.'

'When exactly did this occur, Miss Tyson?'

'Well, let's see,' pondered Stella. 'It was last week – yes, Tuesday.'

'And where was this view?'

Stella looked at him blankly.

'View?'

'The view, Miss Tyson,' returned Thorne impatiently. 'The one you and Mr Makepeace stopped to admire.'

Stella looked a little irritated, as if she couldn't see the point of this line of questioning. But she replied confidently:

'Well, we'd had lunch in Wendover. The view was about a mile south of it on the London road. I remember it especially because Charley pointed out to me the house where Daisy Wilson, the playwright, once lived. It was a folly shaped like a pyramid.'

Thorne nodded.

'I see, Miss Tyson, thank you very much. We won't trouble you any more today.'

'Really?' asked Stella hopefully. 'If you'd like to know the name of the restaurant in Wendover – '

'No, it won't be necessary just now. We'll be in touch with you again if we think you can help.'

At this Thorne rose and nodded at Ballantyne who also rose.

The two policemen left the building and walked in silence to their car. Thorne was asking himself what he'd found out. It was, he'd learned long ago, the indirect things which mattered. It was not so much the answers that witnesses gave as the little movements they made when giving them. It was their glances, the way their eyes contracted, the hesitations, the slips – these were what ultimately put you on the track of the truth even when a witness was not deliberately lying.

The fact was that witnesses always knew more than they were conscious of knowing. Thorne believed in getting at this buried truth.

So what had Stella told him that she didn't know she'd told him? What had he learned from Mrs Makepeace that the lady hadn't realized she could teach him?

But Thorne also knew that it would be fruitless to search too hard. It was better to let what he had heard settle into his own subconscious mind. Then, on some future day, in some unknown place, something that he had already learned would become clear to him.

'Where to now, sir?' asked Ballantyne.

'Straight up to the T-junction,' said Thorne. 'After that, I'll direct you.'

They drove in silence for a while. Thorne realized that Ballantyne was respecting his mental privacy. He smiled faintly. A courteous young man was Sergeant Ballantyne. But would he prove a good copper? Had he the nose, the flair, the instinct?

'Did you believe her, sir?' Ballantyne asked finally. 'When she said the deceased proposed to her?'

'Let's avoid euphemisms, sergeant,' advised Thorne gruffly. 'Corpses or bodies but no deceased.'

'I'm sorry, sir,' said Ballantyne.

Thorne pointed.

'Just past the baker's van. First right.'

'Yes, sir,' said Ballantyne, and he made the required turn.

'Alright, let's recap,' said Thorne. 'Mrs Makepeace told us her husband was finished with his mistress. But according to the mistress she and Makepeace had lunch together last Tuesday.'

Thorne paused, hoping that Ballantyne would take

up the tale. To his satisfaction, the young sergeant obliged.

'And that same night, according to Mrs Makepeace, their home was broken into and poison was put in the flask.'

'Which would mean,' specified Thorne, 'that both ladies could have been telling the truth. Improbable in the nature of things but not, I suppose, impossible.'

At this point, Ballantyne surprised his chief with quite an impressive deduction.

'It hangs together in another way too, sir,' he pointed out. 'Mrs Makepeace said her husband couldn't face a meal out. Well, if he'd had a heavy lunch with his mistress, arranged to marry her and perhaps celebrated with a – well, a spot of hanky-panky, he might well have been too tired.'

'Stop, sergeant,' ordered Thorne.

'You disagree, sir?' asked Ballantyne anxiously.

'No,' snapped Thorne, 'stop the bloody car.'

Ballantyne immediately pulled up at the curb.

'Who are we checking out?' he asked curiously.

He saw that they had stopped in a rather shabby street lined on both sides with shops and small businesses.

Thorne chuckled.

'We're not. We're having lunch. Do you like Greek food, sergeant?'

He perceived that Ballantyne sounded a little uncertain when he said:

'It can be tasty, sir.'

'It can,' Thorne said sternly, 'be pure poetry, as I think you'll agree when you've tasted Costa's dolmades. And you won't snitch if we wash them down with a bottle of retsina, will you, sergeant?'

Ballantyne contented himself with grinning as the two officers got out of their car and crossed the road towards the small, seedy-looking restaurant that, Thorne knew, served some of the finest Greek food in London.

6

Nina Latimer had been Charles Makepeace's secretary. Thorne knew that secretaries sometimes know more about their employers than wives, mothers or children. Consequently an interview with Nina was high on his list of priorities. After lunch, which Ballantyne, surprising himself, had thoroughly enjoyed, the two detectives returned to Carr Sillmann to interview the dead man's personal secretary.

Thorne knew that the lady was middle-aged but had expected her to be smart and rather glamorous with it. She proved to be not unattractive but her dress was if anything a little dowdy and the adjective that came first to Thorne's mind when he interviewed her in her small but well-equipped office was 'motherly'.

'You were fond of Mr Makepeace?' Thorne asked mildy, although aware of the hidden force of the question.

Nina immediately rewarded him with a revealing slip of the tongue.

'Well, we'd been together – ' she began and then blushed visibly and tried again. 'That is, I'd worked for Mr Makepeace for twenty-three years.'

'I believe you're a widow, Mrs Latimer?' explored Thorne further.

Nina picked up the implication immediately.

'I really don't see – ' she bridled.

Thorne interrupted sharply.

'It's my job to find out who killed Mr Makepeace.'

And then Nina surprised him.

'I know who killed him,' she said.

Thorne looked at her in astonishment.

'Do you?' he asked.

'Yes,' said Nina firmly. 'It was whoever has been persecuting him with threatening phone calls.'

'I see,' said Thorne. 'And for how long has he been receiving threatening phone calls?'

'Well, for at least a year,' replied Nina.

'And did Mr Makepeace discuss these calls with you?'

'No, but I heard them – or at least his end of them – several times on my intercom. I could tell he was very upset by them.'

'So these calls were on his private line?' asked Thorne.

'Yes.'

'Doesn't that mean they must have been from someone he knew well?'

'Normally it would,' agreed Nina. 'But you see sometimes people called him at home during office hours and then his wife might give them his private number here. It annoyed him.'

Thorne exchanged a quick glance with Ballantyne. This information confirmed what they had inferred about the relationship betwen the Makepeaces. Thorne then turned to Nina again.

'Mrs Latimer, would you have the times of any of these calls? Preferably the exact times?'

Nina nodded.

'Yes, the last one anyway. I know because it happened just before I went home on the night Mr Makepeace was killed. That would have been five-twenty-five P.M.. Is that exact enough for you?'

'It is indeed,' said the superintendent enthusiastically.

A little later, as he and Ballantyne left the Carr Sillmann building, Thorne was turning over in his mind the possibility that an abusive phone call was what had made Charles Makepeace turn to his whisky flask that night. Moreover the call might have been made in order to do just that. But who had made it?

After interviewing Nina, Thorne and Ballantyne parted company. Thorne went to interview Charles Makepeace's solicitor about the dead man's will. Ballantyne went to question Makepeace's doctor. Thorne travelled by taxi and Ballantyne, since he was going further, took the car.

Ballantyne drove to Wimpole Street where Doctor Terence O'Malley had his consulting rooms. The appointment had been made in advance but nevertheless Ballantyne was kept waiting for nearly half an hour.

Then he was ushered by a lady receptionist into a first floor office which was furnished in red plush and looked more like a sitting room than a doctor's surgery.

Dr O'Malley, a tall and plump man with a round head and small features, sat behind an enormous desk. He proved to have a slight Irish accent.

'You want to know about Charles Makepeace?' he asked, turning through a large medical file on his desk.

'That's right,' returned Ballantyne. 'You were his doctor, I believe, sir.'

'One of them,' corrected O'Malley. 'He also had a GP. I'm a heart man basically. But I'd known Charles for many years. We were friends. I had a listen to his poor old ticker once a year.'

'And when was the last such check-up?' asked Ballantyne.

'In April. It was always April. But his heart was no joke.'

The remark, presumably a reference to April Fool's day, seemed to Ballantyne in dubious taste.

'Could you tell me about it?' he asked.

O'Malley obliged in thoughtful detail. Ballantyne learned that the consultant had warned Makepeace at his last examination that his heart was in very bad condition. O'Malley had told him further that if he did not give up alcohol completely he would not live long.

'And how did that affect him?' asked Ballantyne.

O'Malley smiled.

'He promised he'd give up the booze.'

'And do you think he meant it?' asked Ballantyne.

'Well, of course he meant it,' returned the consultant a trifle irritably. 'He always meant it.'

Ballantyne frowned a little.

'What do you mean by that?' he asked.

O'Malley shook his head with a grim smile.

'Well, I'd been telling him the same thing every year for the past three years. And every year when I told him, it scared him silly. But in my opinion he always started hitting the bottle again after a few days.'

'And do you think that's what happened this year too?' asked Ballantyne.

'I understand he drank poisoned whisky? Doesn't that suggest it?' asked the doctor soberly.

After leaving O'Malley's consulting room, Ballantyne drove back to the City. When he reached Thorne's office in Wood Street he found that his boss had not yet returned from seeing the solicitor. He then phoned Carr Sillmann to find out if John Field would be available later that afternoon, since Thorne wanted to ask him some additional questions.

To his astonishment he found that the young banker

had been invalided home. It seemed he had been injured in a demonstration outside a chemical works. This demonstration had been organized by local people protesting about alleged pollution by a firm that Carr Sillmann were representing in a takeover battle: Dinslow Chemicals. John Field had gone out of London to observe the demonstration and see if he could spot any signs of dirty tricks. He had apparently been involved in a scuffle. For all that, it seemed he was not badly hurt, but his doctor had advised him to stay at home for a day or two.

Hearing this, Ballantyne took it upon himself to obtain Field's number from the merchant bank and to phone him at home. The phone was answered by Mrs Field who assured the sergeant that John was able to see them if they were prepared to drive out to their Surrey address. Ballantyne thanked her and said he would let her know what his superior decided. He was still on the phone when Thorne arrived back in his office.

Thorne listened to the end of the conversation and, when it was over, he asked:

'What was that all about?'

Ballantyne explained the situation.

'Long drive,' said Thorne when Ballantyne had finished. 'And we haven't got much to ask him. Just a few details of office routine. On the other hand these violent demos are interesting. Sir Max said that dirty tricks haven't reached the stage of homicide yet. But Field seems to be in a good position to comment on that. I think we'd better go.'

In the car, Thorne questioned Ballantyne about his visit to the doctor and Ballantyne told him what O'Malley had said.

'So,' said Thorne thoughtfully. 'Every year his consultant warned him off the booze and every year he drank tea for a week or two before going back on the hard stuff. And this year seems to have been no different.'

'If it had been,' Ballantyne supplemented, 'he wouldn't have been at his whisky flask, would he? But we know both from what Stella Tyson said and the fact that he took the poison that he was using it regularly.'

'Right,' agreed Thorne. 'Which means O'Malley's warning doesn't come into it.'

'What did the lawyer say, sir?' asked Ballantyne.

'Nothing startling about the will,' returned Thorne. 'The bulk of the estate to his wife and a substantial bequest to Stella Tyson.'

'But doesn't that tend to confirm what Stella Tyson said?' asked Ballantyne with a hint of excitement.

'Not really,' said Thorne. 'The will was made a long time ago. It could simply mean that Makepeace never got around to changing it. He was careless about financial details. You often find that with bankers and accountants. The same way with mechanics who drive broken-down cars. They get enough of their trade during working hours.'

'Fascinating, sir,' said Ballantyne. Then he added mischievously, 'Or is that another example of trying to seem more perceptive than you really are?'

Thorne grinned.

'You decide, sergeant.'

A little later they turned into the paved courtyard of a converted farmhouse and pulled up in front of the trim building. A pretty little girl was skipping outside the door. They smiled at her and she nodded politely.

Thorne rang the bell. It was soon answered by a small attractive woman.

'Superintendent Thorne and Sergeant Ballantyne,' said Thorne apologetically. 'But if it's inconvenient – ?'

'No, it's alright,' said the woman, who the detective realized must be Mrs Field. 'John's quite prepared to see you. Actually he wanted to go to work but I wouldn't let him.'

'He's not – '

'Oh no, he's not seriously injured. Just a bit battered. Superficial contusions, but a lot of them.'

'You sound like a doctor,' said Thorne, who knew perfectly well that she was one.

She nodded.

'I am – paediatrician – children.'

She ushered the two men into a somewhat self-consciously rustic, but attractive, living room. A few minutes later John Field, wearing a dressing gown over pyjamas, and with several conspicuous bruises on his face, appeared.

'Sorry about this,' he said with a deprecating smile.

'Not at all, sir. Sorry you've been damaged. Riot, was it?'

'Demonstration outside a chemical works. Dirty tricks, in my opinion.'

John elaborated briefly. There had been a series of demonstrations outside plants belonging to Dinslow Chemicals. Such events were, of course, not uncommon outside any chemical works since chemicals ranked second only to nuclear installations in their power to mobilize anxiety and protest. But Field had an idea that this particular series of demonstrations might not be unconnected with the forthcoming take-over battle. His theory was based chiefly on the fact

53

that photographs of several of the demos had revealed that a tall lean man, apparently just one of the demonstrators, had been present at plants hundreds of miles apart. The clear implication seemed to be that someone might be organizing the events.

Thorne was interested. He knew that as the stakes continually rose, so dirty tricks got ever dirtier. A whole new branch of criminology had grown up devoted to crimes connected with industry. These ranged from simple snooping to assassination.

Field suddenly screwed up his eyes as if in pain and raised his hand towards his head.

'Are you alright, sir?' asked the superintendent.

'Headache,' returned the other ruefully. 'Got clouted with something – brick I think.'

'Well, we won't keep you any longer,' said Thorne, nodding at Ballantyne.

7

Thorne and Ballantyne drove back to London. They travelled in silence for a while. Then Ballantyne asked tentatively: 'Do you fancy him, sir?'

Thorne shook his head.

'Never did.'

'He has no alibi for either the time of the phone call or the time of the break-in,' offered Ballantyne. 'And isn't it a bit odd that he returned to Carr Sillmann on the night of the murder?'

Thorne said:

'Perhaps. But it's a bit of a boggler to suppose he just strolled into Makepeace's office and poured poison into his hip flask. On the other hand, he does seem to attract violence. He was near Makepeace the night he died. And now he's got himself duffed up in some dirty tricks punch-up. We'd better keep an eye on him. Now who else have we got?'

'The guru,' said Ballantyne positively. 'The astrologer.'

Thorne smiled.

'He's the one you fancy, isn't he?'

Ballantyne shrugged.

'Well – not exactly, sir. But we do know he and Makepeace hated each other – jealous of each other's influence on Sir Max, as far as I can make out.'

The 'guru' was a man called Musquat Singh. He was a professional astrologer who was retained, at what was rumoured to be an astronomical sum, by Carr Sillman. This fact was famous throughout the City and anyone who showed any tendency to jeer when they were told about it was soon silenced by a simple recitation of the merchant bank's trading profits over the years. Of course, not many people believed in supernatural influence on world trade, but everyone believed in making money. Whatever else he was, Musquat Singh was no enemy to Carr Sillmann's profit margins. No-one knew how seriously Max Sillmann took the advice of his house astrologer but everyone respected Sir Max's financial acumen.

Thorne had not yet interviewed Musquat Singh. He had not been able to. Singh was currently in the United States attending a world conference of astrologers. Thorne himself considered astrology to be nonsense but he had not been surprised to learn of Sir Max's devotion to it. In his experience a lot of powerful men had a strong streak of superstition in their natures. During Thorne's first interview with Sir Max he had questioned the banker about the place of Musquat Singh in his organization, asking, amongst other things:

'Do you believe in astrology, sir?'

'If you are asking,' Sir Max had replied thoughtfully, 'whether I believe that lumps of rock millions of miles away can influence human affairs on this planet I can only reply that it seems to me improbable. Nevertheless – do you understand the universe, superintendent?'

Thorne shook his head.

'No, I don't, sir.'

The banker smiled.

'Most people are not so honest. But the fact is that even scientists only understand fragments of it. The world we experience is like a campfire in a great forest. Some people perceive that all is dark beyond the little circle of light and they live in awe. Others are quite at home. They are called materialists.'

'Most people consider bankers to be materialists,' Thorne had been bold enough to observe.

Sir Max shook his head.

'A vulgar error. What is most real to most people? Money. But only bankers know that it is nothing – lumps of inert metal, bits of paper, at bottom simply an agreement to ascribe value to that which has none. Only bankers know how billions can vanish from a balance sheet and, after the right incantations, reappear on another. You see, superintendent, only bankers can see through the walls of money.'

Thorne himself was a materialist. He had no time for psi or ESP or astrology. He believed in a concrete world and in cause and effect. He believed that a detective must be a materialist or else he would founder in a maze of false trails. But he also believed in intuition. He assumed that in his case the word was simply shorthand for an immeasurably rapid sifting of evidence, but he knew it could not be weighed in scales or detected with IQ tests. Some coppers had it and some didn't.

Thorne held no superstitious beliefs. But he did not underestimate their power. He knew, for example, that much of Indian industry and commerce depended on astrology and that Indian industry and commerce were highly successful. He knew that some scientists were spiritualists. He knew that some police forces consulted clairvoyants. He knew that oil companies employed dowsers. He was not inclined to scoff.

Since that conversation with Sir Max he had made inquiries about Carr Sillmann's reputation. Did other city institutions regard Sir Max as a crank? The answer seemed to be: yes they did. But a successful one. And success, in the City, transcended all other considerations. In the last resort, people felt, Sir Max listened to Musquat Singh only when the astrologer's views tallied with his own. Otherwise he went his own way.

Musquat Singh was a prime suspect because it was common knowledge that he and Charles had each been jealous of the other's influence on the head of Carr Sillmann.

Thorne arrived home to find Milly ironing his shirts in the well-equipped kitchen of their town house. There was no need for Milly to iron shirts. There was no need for her to shop or clean or cook. Even with the contemporary difficulty of finding servants Milly's money could readily have procured them. Indeed the Thorne's had several part-time servants – women who came in and cleaned and men who came and gardened. There were others too who came in only on special occasions such as cocktail or dinner parties. But Milly did a great deal of the housework herself and she did it, as she told Thorne, because she loved him and wanted to be a real wife to him. It didn't interfere with her social round. It didn't prevent her from playing tennis or riding. For whatever else anyone might have said about Milly, and few people said anything very nasty, she had an abundance of energy. As soon as Thorne entered the kitchen Milly left her ironing, ran to him and kissed him.

'Lance? You're not mad at me, are you?' she asked.

He sighed, went to the electric kettle and put it on. He reached out to the mug tree, and got himself a mug for coffee. He asked her:

'Would you like a coffee?'

'No thanks,' she replied, going back to her ironing. 'I had tea about half an hour ago. Lance, don't be mad.'

'I'm trying not to be,' he said, getting down the

Nescafé. 'But I really thought we'd agreed that you wouldn't call me except in matters of great urgency.'

It had happened a couple of hours earlier. She had called Thorne at work. He had been interviewing Dan Maitland, not a suspect, but someone who, Thorne hoped, might give him fresh information about Carr Sillmann. Maitland had been doing just that when Milly had rung. She had phoned to ask Thorne if he liked Queen Anne. It had taken him a moment to realize that she was talking about architecture and then he had admitted that he had only a hazy idea of what Queen Anne architecture was like, but he had no objection to it. After that, and with a barely civil 'good-bye', he had quickly hung up the phone.

'Lance,' protested Milly, setting the iron on its heel and going towards him at the table where he'd seated himself with his coffee, 'I couldn't just plonk down half a million without knowing if you liked Queen Anne.'

She leaned down and kissed him on his left ear. She knew he liked being kissed on his left ear. He stood up to avoid succumbing to this unfair mode of argument.

'I didn't know you intended to buy a house today,' he said.

'I didn't,' protested Milly. 'But it turned out to be such a bargain. Honest, Lance, it'll make the perfect weekend cottage.'

'Good,' said Thorne. 'Well, I hope you have a lot of lovely weekends there.'

'We'll both have lovely weekends there,' enthused Milly; 'if the sun shines.'

'You still haven't got the message, have you, Milly,' said Thorne a trifle bitterly. 'I am not going to have time for weekends in the country.'

'But why not?' she demanded.

'Because,' explained Thorne patiently, 'as I have told you many times before, I intend to be the top cop in this country one day.'

'Okay,' said Milly fiercely. 'I'll be Mrs Top Cop. But money and the things it buys never hurt an ambitious man's chances.'

'That's where you're wrong,' expostulated Thorne. 'Money, as it happens, is not an infallible route to success in the police force. And when it's linked with a dizzy girl who's always getting into trouble – '

He broke off. They looked at each other in silence for a moment. She appeared genuinely hurt. She said quietly:

'Is that really all I am to you, Lance? Just a dizzy girl?'

'Well,' began Thorne, but then he sighed again. 'No, of course it's not all you are to me, Milly. But I do wish you could resign yourself to being a policeman's wife because I can't settle down to being a rich girl's – '

'What?' cried Milly furiously. 'Plaything? Gigolo? Why you goddamn – '

For some reason her anger always triggered a nervous impulse to laugh in Thorne. He began to grin broadly. She advanced on him with clenched fists. He knew she was quite capable of punching him on the chest and even on the face. He raised his hands to ward her off.

'Sorry, sorry,' he apologized. 'Alright, then, girl, tell me about our new country cottage – is it bigger or smaller than Versailles?'

The next day, Thorne and Milly went shopping in Bond Street. While they were doing so an incident occurred which seemed to Thorne to confirm his worst suspicions about the dangers of being married to a rich – but dizzy – girl.

They were looking for furniture for the Queen Anne manor house which Milly had bought. She had promised Thorne that she would conclude all the legal transactions and have the place furnished and ready for a summer party, which would double as a birthday party for Thorne, on the 27th of August. He did not think it possible to complete the complex formalities in time but Milly had no doubts at all about her ability to do so. Needless to say Thorne was far from overjoyed at the prospect of spending half the day shopping. He had better things to do and almost all of them were connected with the Makepeace case.

On the other hand, in spite of his protests to Milly, he knew that he was bound to spend some of his time in the twelve-bedroomed 'country cottage' and, in spite of his pose of being just a simple country boy with no taste or knowledge about art, in fact he had very decided views about such matters. If furniture and paintings and such things needed to be bought Thorne felt it was prudent to be in at the buying.

Milly had come home once with a work of art by a modern master, a young woman, which had consisted of arrangements of wavy black and white lines which it had made Thorne literally sea-sick to contemplate. He had acknowledged that it had considerable power but he had flatly refused to live with the optical monster. Milly must not be allowed to fill the country cottage with such daunting objects.

So they went to Tellers, the largest and most prestigious antique dealer in Bond Street. They bought a number of items before coming upon, in a back room on the ground floor, a huge oak dining table. It must have been thirty feet long and looked as if it might easily once have graced a baronial hall.

Thorne gave it scarcely a glance but Milly stopped transfixed.

'That's it!' she exclaimed. 'That's exactly what we need for the main dining room.'

'How many dining rooms are there?' asked Thorne mildly.

'Two,' said Milly, 'or three if you include the little breakfast room next to the kitchen.'

'And one of them's big enough for that thing?' asked Thorne impressed.

'Easily. It's just right. Of course, I don't expect to use it for meals. You could seat fifty round that table but it will be great for buffets and we can put those big Chinese jars on it. How much do you suppose they want for it?'

Thorne laid small claim to being a judge of the value of antiques. He shrugged.

'A couple of thousand?' he suggested.

Milly laughed.

'Lance, it's seventeenth century. It would be a snip at twenty thousand. Hang on, I'll just go and ask someone.'

She hurried away and Thorne went for a short walk round the table. It was indeed an impressive object. If its sides had been walled it would have made a snug but acceptable little apartment. As he was contemplating it a man, some fifteen years older than he, passed by with a lady. The man started perceptibly on seeing him.

'Lance!' he exclaimed.

Thorne turned and recognized Assistant Commissioner Halpern of Scotland Yard. He immediately felt alert and ice-cold as he did whenever there was danger. He smiled.

'Hello, sir – Mrs Halpern?'

'This is unexpected,' beamed the assistant commissioner. 'Looking for stolen goods, I suppose?'

This was a reasonable assumption. The senior officer knew Thorne only as a promising junior officer in the City force and had no knowledge of his glittering marriage. Thorne had a feeling that it would be unwise to disclose the true nature or purpose of his visit. On the other hand, he didn't want to lie to a senior officer. He took refuge in stammering:

'Well – er – that is, sir – I'm just here to – '

Happily the assistant commissioner was eager to convey news of his own and failed to notice Thorne's consternation.

'Now we're just doing a spot of shopping,' he confided. 'Last year, Lance, I'd never have dreamed of entering a place like this. But since my promotion – well, you'll never believe it but we've bought a chair.'

He pointed to the adjoining room where quite a handsome leather chair could be seen. Thorne gazed at it with what he hoped would look like profound admiration.

'Really, sir?' he said. 'Looks a fine piece.'

Mrs Halpern, who came originally from Birmingham and retained traces of the region's accent, added proudly.

'It's eighteenth century – probably made by Dyson.'

Thorne said inquiringly:

'Dyson? I'm afraid I don't know all the names.'

Halpern smiled in a superior way.

'Hardly surprising, Lance. Takes years to get a grip on antiques. Now that chair set us back nearly nine thousand pounds – but it will give our home a touch of class.'

Thorne nodded.

'No doubt about that, sir.'

And it was at this point that Milly came flying back, breathless and excited. Sensing danger, Thorne attempted to deflect whatever message she might be bringing.

'Assistant Commissioner Halpern,' he explained hastily, 'and Mrs Halpern. Commissioner, this is my wife, Milly.'

Halpern nodded. He looked a trifle surprised by Milly's youthfulness.

'Hello, Mrs Thorne,' he said in a friendly enough way. 'So you've been shopping too, eh? Seen anything you fancy?'

'Right. This table,' exclaimed Milly enthusiastically. She turned eagerly to Thorne. 'Darling, it's only seven thousand. Of course a set of matching chairs will double that – but what a bargain!'

Thorne smiled in what he hoped was an indulgent way, intending to convey to the Halperns that Milly often suffered from these delusions of grandeur. But he could tell it was no use. The smiles froze on their faces. The assistant commissioner nodded stonily.

'Well, I'll leave you to your shopping then,' he said.

They turned and marched off.

Thorne didn't reproach Milly. He realized she was not to blame for the gaffe. She was merely excited by the furniture and she had behaved with the naturalness of a child. But he was convinced that such episodes did him professional harm. This was strange, for Thorne was a good psychologist. Indeed his rapid rise in the police service had been chiefly dependent on that quality. But he was also a boy from a humble background, deeply imbued with the protestant work ethic, who believed that the only way to rise was through endeavour and efficiency.

However, in spite of Thorne's resolve not to reproach Milly for the scene with Assistant Commissioner Halpern, Thorne could not help brooding about it and Milly sensed this. That evening as they prepared dinner together she asked him if he was upset about anything. He returned more of a grunt than a reply. She then said pathetically:

'But I don't understand, Lance. What's the matter?'

Thorne sighed.

'Thorsten Veblen,' he said cryptically. 'Have you ever heard of Thorsten Veblen?'

Milly had been to Vassar and UCL, but there were gaps in her education.

'The racing driver?' she asked hopefully.

Thorne snorted. 'The philosopher! He wrote a seminal book called "The Theory of the Leisure Class". It was about you, Milly, or people like you.'

'Oh, Lance, even poor people have parties.' his wife replied.

'Not with marquees and caterers and a guest-list of hundreds.'

'But, Lance, I'll handle everything. You've never had a proper birthday party and we must have a warming for the cottage.'

'It's simply impossible,' protested Thorne. 'It's only six weeks to my birthday.'

'I'll make it,' said Milly confidently. 'When I hustle I really go.'

'But, Milly, the legal formalities – '

'Bullshit, Lance. I'm rich, remember? I've got a top solicitor. I can buy speed.'

Thorne knew this was true but there were other objections.

'Anyway,' he said, 'I couldn't commit myself. My case-load –'

'Oh, I know about case-loads, Lance. The higher you get the bigger the load you carry. That's what my dad always used to say. So don't promise a thing, Lance. Some of us are having a swell party. If you can look in for a drink, we'd all love to see you.'

She smiled at him affectionately. Her good humour was irresistible. He smiled back.

'I'll be there,' he said.

8

Thorne was five minutes late getting to work the next morning because of a hold-up on the underground. These days he always went to the office by underground. For some time, after first taking over the City job, he had driven to work. But that took him through the centre of London's West End and heavy traffic. He had tried detouring North and he had tried detouring South but the journey always seemed to take about the same time. He had even tried riding a bicycle, which did indeed cut his travelling time. But it was distinctly unpleasant riding a bike in a smog of exhaust fumes. So in the end he had settled for the underground which took him almost from door to door.

This morning the train had stopped in the tunnel. It hadn't been especially crowded and there had seemed no reason for the hold-up. It had only remained motionless for about ten minutes and then started up again. But the delay was just enough to make Thorne a little late.

Ballantyne was waiting in his office and Thorne sensed at once that he had important news.

'Get it out,' said Thorne, turning quickly through his letters.

'Nina phoned – you know, Makepeace's secretary at Carr Sillmann,' said Ballantyne eagerly. 'She wasn't very clear, but it was something about having found a tape with the murderer's voice on it.'

'Now that would be a breakthrough,' said Thorne, impressed. 'Let's get over there and see if it's true.'

Less than twenty minutes later, the two detectives were seated in Nina's small office at Carr Sillmann, watching her set up a cassette recorder linked to a concealed speaker in her desk. Thorne noted that her desk was piled with files, both electronic and the outmoded paper kind. He guessed that faithful Nina was still engaged in sorting through Charles Makepeace's professional effects. Thorne was sure that she was performing this task as a labour of love and that her dedication to it was what had turned up – well, whatever it was that had turned up.

'Alright,' said Nina, and her excitement was obvious. 'Are you ready?'

'Quite ready, Mrs Latimer,' said Thorne, encouragingly.

Nina turned and, with a faint smile of triumph, punched a button. For a moment there was nothing. And then there was a voice saying:

'You're forgetting the estate management aspect which – '

This voice was interrupted by another one saying:

'I'm not forgetting anything, Mr Makepeace – if you'll just wait – '

Thorne realized that the first voice was that of Charles Makepeace. This was interesting although the conversation was not. For a while the inconsequential exchange went on. The second speaker was clearly an accountant. Then, with nothing of obvious significance having been said, Nina reached forwards and hit the 'off' button. Thorne and Ballantyne exchanged a puzzled glance.

Nina turned to them again. She was blushing with embarrassment.

'I was sure that that was the right place – but it can't

have been, can it?' she stammered. 'I'm so sorry, gentlemen.'

'It's alright,' said Thorne encouragingly. 'Don't upset yourself, Mrs Latimer. We've got plenty of time.'

Nina turned to some notes in a note-book. She looked at some numbers she'd written. She looked back at the tape recorder. She spent perhaps another two minutes adjusting the machine. She turned back to them.

'Well, I think this must be it,' she said at last. 'Anyway, we'd better try.'

She turned again and punched the 'on' button. Once more, Thorne and Ballantyne heard Charles Makepeace talking.

'The entire stock of assets taken into account might just – '

At this point there was a faint, almost soundless thud indicating that the tape recorder had switched into another mode. For a split second after that there was nothing. And then there was something shocking. Thorne, more experienced and disciplined than his younger sergeant, did not move. But Ballantyne actually jumped slightly as a woman's voice screamed: 'Murderer! He'd be alive today if it weren't for you – you murderer!' This scream of hate was followed almost immediately by the voice of Charles Makepeace once more only this time that voice was distorted with anger and fear.

'For God's sake, Mrs T – '

And then once more there was the faint thud of the tape recorder switching modes and the accountant came back on, saying:

'Even if we could raise that much in – '

And then Nina switched off the machine, turned

and gazed at the detectives with an expression of triumph.

'Alright – who was it?' asked Thorne, very quietly and calmly.

Nina shook her head.

'I've no idea.'

'How did it get on the tape?' asked Thorne.

Nina explained: 'I can't be certain. But my guess is that it was accidental. Mr Makepeace had a button for recording incoming telephone messages if he wanted to. He sometimes touched it accidentally.'

Thorne nodded.

'Yes, we obviously heard a fragment of a longer exchange. Anyway, I'm very grateful, Mrs Latimer. Now, if you could let me have that tape I'll get it to our acoustics people.'

Nina nodded and started removing the tape from the machine. As she did so, she said with surprising ferocity:

'You heard what Mr Makepeace called her? That mad woman? It was a name beginning with "T".'

Thorne nodded and smiled a trifle grimly.

'You should be a detective, Mrs Latimer,' he said. 'Thank you very much.'

It wasn't until the next day that Thorne and Ballantyne had a copy of the tape which they could play to various people for possible identification. The original, of course, was too precious to be used for such a purpose and was by then firmly lodged in the police acoustics laboratory and very exacting tests were being made on it. The detectives took the copy to Sir Max's office and played it to him. He was appalled and astonished. Thorne was satisfied that he was also completely baffled by what he heard. From Sir Max's office, they went to a small conference room which had been put at their disposal, where they had arranged to meet John Field – who was now back at work.

Thorne made sure they arrived a few minutes before Field was due. He intended to stage the experiment very carefully. He stationed Ballantyne by the tape machine. He sat at the far end of the table from Ballantyne and pretended to be studying a file. But John Field did not arrive on time and ten minutes later the disgruntled detectives were still waiting for him.

John had not forgotten about the appointment. A little earlier he had glanced at his desk diary and then at his watch and decided he should leave to meet Thorne and Ballantyne in the conference room in a very few minutes. But just about then, Diana, his secretary, phoned through on the internal line to tell him that Colin Tucker had called unexpectedly and would like to see him.

Tucker was the owner and managing director of a small firm specializing in industrial pollutants. The firm worked chiefly as consultants to industry but was also useful to investors and financial institutions. Carr Sillmann sometimes used Tucker's services and now, with a takeover struggle impending between two chemical firms, it seemed clear to John that Colin might easily prove useful.

Field had known Colin Tucker, exclusively in his professional capacity, for some years but he knew that Charles Makepeace had been a very old friend of his. Indeed he had an idea that Makepeace had helped Colin to start his firm a decade or so back.

John glanced at his watch. He could, he decided, spare Colin two minutes which was as much as anyone could reasonably expect if they called unannounced on a frantic young merchant banker. He asked Diana to

71

wheel him in and a few minutes later Diana ushered a small thin man with wispy grey hair into John's office.

'Hello, Colin, what can I do for you?' John greeted him cheerfully.

'Just wanted to make sure you were keeping me on file,' the other returned with a faint smile.

'How do you mean?' asked John, puzzled.

'Well, it was always unofficial, wasn't it?' Tucker elaborated. 'I mean, the work we did for you. Just a phone call from poor old Charles and we'd get stuck in. Now that he's gone – ?'

John realized that the little man was asking if his position as consultant was still secure.

'Oh, good Lord, Colin, no need to worry about that. You're the best. Everyone says that you and your lot are tops in the field. We wouldn't dream of using anyone else. Tell you what. I'll make it official, if you like. We'll draw up some form of contract.'

He saw the look of satisfaction on the other's face and realized that this was what he'd been angling for. John hurriedly qualified the offer.

'But not now if you don't mind, Colin. I'll let you have a draft in a day or two. At the moment I have a rather pressing appointment. With two cops actually.'

'Superintendent Thorne and Sergeant Ballantyne?' asked the other ruefully.

John stared at him in surprise.

'Exactly. But how do you – ' and then he understood. 'Don't tell me you're a suspect too, Colin?'

The other nodded.

'Inevitable, I should have thought. I'm a ranking expert on industrial poisons and I knew Charles well.'

'Yes, but you were his best friend and he – well – ' John broke off awkwardly.

'That's right,' Tucker acknowledged his unspoken

remark. 'He was my benefactor. Could never have started my firm without him.'

'Weren't you two in the navy together?' John asked curiously.

Tucker nodded.

'On the same destroyer. Charles was the captain. I was Jimmy, the first officer. The odd thing is that after the war we didn't see each other for about twenty years. And then I bumped into him quite by chance in the City. I'd come here to try and get a loan – met blank walls everywhere. But Charles said: "I'll take care of it." And he did. He got me all the money I needed and later, of course, he put some of his own money into my company. The rotten thing is that he's hardly made a penny out of it so far. We've had a long slow start and we're only just on the edge of the big breakthrough.'

'What kind of breakthrough?' asked John, alert for any news of City matters.

'Signed for a big retainer with Delta just last week. That's why Charles wanted to increase his investment. As a matter of fact he was going to sign it the day after he died. So his death's lost me a good packet of capital I could have used. But we should be alright. With any luck we'll have something for Isobel – '

'His wife?' John interrupted.

'Oh yes. We were mates – all of us. Janet and I would often dine with them and vice versa. In fact, I'm going to feel his loss in a lot of ways.'

John, who found it hard to match Colin Tucker's obvious grief at the loss of his old friend, changed the subject.

'Anyway, Colin, there's no question that we'll continue to use you. As a matter of fact we've got something up your street – '

And at that point, the internal phone rang and Diana told him that the detectives were beginning to fret a little. John glanced at his watch. He saw that he was nearly a quarter of an hour late for his appointment with them.

'Sorry, Colin,' he said, getting to his feet. 'Time and the law wait for no man. But – I'll give you a buzz as soon as we've drawn up a draft agreement.'

Colin Tucker knew the ropes. Nobody could be allowed to remain in a merchant banker's office when he left it. He rose and accompanied John out into the corridor where they parted, Tucker towards the lift and John towards the conference room and the waiting police.

Reaching the conference room, John dashed in, saying apologetically:

'Sorry, gentlemen. Always happens – someone called just as I was setting off.'

He addressed himself to Thorne and nodded civilly at Ballantyne. Thorne stood up.

'Perfectly alright, sir,' he said gruffly. 'I just wanted you to hear something.'

Field looked puzzled.

'Hear something, superintendent?'

Thorne wanted the young man to be relaxed and unsuspecting.

'Yes, just something that might have a bearing on the case. Would you like to sit down here, sir?'

He indicated the chair beside him.

'Of course,' said John Field.

He approached the chair Thorne had indicated and prepared to seat himself. As he began to lower himself, Thorne made a small prearranged signal to Ballantyne. And the latter pressed the 'on' button of the machine, now linked to a powerful speaker. With terrifying impact, the scream of hatred rang round the small conference room:

'Murderer! He'd be alive today if it weren't for you! You murderer!'

Thorne watched Field closely and saw that he froze, half-way to the seat. His head jerked round and he gazed at Ballantyne at the other end of the table with a look of astonishment and dismay. Ballantyne hit the 'off' button immediately the hate scream was over. And Field continued lowering himself on to the seat as he exclaimed:

'What the hell was that?'

No longer easy-going and relaxed, Thorne asked sharply: 'Whose voice was it, Mr Field?'

'What?' asked John blankly.

'Answer my question: who was that woman on the tape?'

'I've no idea,' said John Field. 'Why should I have?'

'Did you recognize the voice?'

'No, certainly not.'

'Think hard,' urged Thorne. 'A woman's voice – hysterical – but you might have heard it before in a calmer mood. Now did you recognize the voice?'

He nodded at Ballantyne who had rewound the tape. Ballantyne once more punched the 'on' button. Again the hate-filled voice, but at somewhat lower volume, sounded in the neat little conference room. And this time, Ballantyne let the tape run on a moment to include Charles Makepeace's truncated reply.

'For God's sake, Mrs T –'

'Well?' asked Thorne.

John looked at him with a bewildered expression.

'I don't understand. The second voice was Charles! But Charles wasn't the murderer. He was the victim. Why did that woman call him a murderer?'

Thorne was satisfied. Field had no knowledge of the woman or her stern accusation.

Thorne sighed:

'We only have the one syllable,' he said. 'Something like Tyn. Our acoustics lab thinks the name was something like Tinsley or Tyndall. Does that ring any bells?'

Field shook his head.

'No, I don't think – ' but then he paused.

Tyndall? Yes, it did ring a bell. But –

Thorne noticed his reaction.

'Yes? What have you got?' he asked urgently.

And then John remembered.

At an interview that afternoon with Morrison, the managing director of Dinslow, he had informed the latter that he intended to pay a visit to Norfolk to interview a man called Nathaniel Mustard. During the riot outside the Dinslow plant Dan had found an envelope with that name and an address on it. John didn't want the police to know this. He wanted to find out himself if Mustard was the organizer of the demonstrations at Dinslow Plants. But when he had told Morrison about this, Morrison said something which now came back to him.

'Yes, I've remembered.' he informed Thorne. 'It's nothing to do with Charles. It's just that earlier today I was talking to the managing director of Dinslow Chemicals and he mentioned a – well – a kind of chemical waste dump in Norfolk. For some reason it's known as Tyndall's Pond.'

Thorne and Ballantyne exchanged a glance.

'Thank you, sir,' said Thorne. 'We'll check that out at once.'

9

The butler said:

'Lady Susan Ross and Mr Daniel Maitland.'

Thorne, surprising himself by the undisciplined movement, turned his head sharply. Yes, it was the young American he'd twice already interviewed at Carr Sillmann. Oh well, it had been bound to happen sooner or later. Once in an idle moment he'd done some mental arithmetic as to the chances of his professional life and his social life overlapping. He had decided that the chances were quite high, about ten per cent in any given year. But somehow until this moment it had never actually happened. After his initial reaction, Thorne went on chatting with his companion, Lady Darius, about the decline of grouse on Scottish grouse moors. But he also made a point of listening to the exchange between their hostess, Lucy Simons, and the new arrivals.

'Dan! Susan!' Mrs Simons exclaimed. 'I didn't know you two were together.'

'Just good friends,' replied Dan Maitland with a rather forced laugh.

The girl said bitchily, 'Don't exaggerate, Dan.'

Dan returned: 'No punch-ups in public, pet.'

At this point, Lucy Simons tried to truncate the burgeoning quarrel.

'Squabbling already?' she said reproachfully. 'Stop it at once and come and meet the others.'

She led the new arrivals to the four guests already present. They were seated near the fireplace in the large, elegant Belgravia drawing room. Lance and the other man stood up.

'Lord and Lady Darius,' she murmured, indicating the standing man and Thorne's seated companion. There were nods and smiles. Then Lucy brought the young couple to Thorne. Before she could say anything, Dan Maitland stopped dead and stared at Lance in amazement. Involuntarily he exclaimed:

'Hey, you're the cop!'

Lucy Simons, mistaking his outburst for youthful mischief, exclaimed severely:

'Now, Daniel, please – '

But Maitland was too excited to be silenced.

'But he's a plain-clothes cop!' he exclaimed. 'He's been hanging around our place trying to sniff out a killer.'

'Dan! Stop this at once,' Lucy said sternly. 'Lance is an old friend. He's Milly's husband and Milly is Patrick Cardington's daughter.' Maitland gazed from Milly to Lance in astonishment. 'It's absolutely incredible,' he exclaimed.

Thorne felt it was time to try and ease the situation. He said softly:

'Try and come to terms with it, old chap. Milly is very rich and I'm a superintendent of detectives. An unlikely combination, perhaps, but not, as you see, impossible.'

It worked. Dan Maitland spread out his hands in apology.

'Hell, I'm sorry. I shouldn't – it's just that it seemed so weird.'

Thorne relaxed, thinking the bumpy patch had been successfully negotiated. Almost immediately he was proved wrong. It seemed that Maitland's companion,

Lady Susan Ross, had something disagreeable to contribute.

'Actually they are a surprising couple, Dan,' she proclaimed, and the hint of malice in her voice was unmistakable. 'The story of how they got together is out of this world. Go on, Milly, tell him about it.'

Oh dear, thought Lance, they know each other. Now what? But Milly, Thorne was glad to observe, looked equal to the situation.

'This is hardly the time, is it, Susan?' she asked.

'Oh, but why not,' Susan Ross exclaimed. 'It's so crashingly romantic – pure Eleanour Glyn.' She spoke to the company at large. 'He rescued her, you see. From kidnappers. On Corsica.' Then she turned to Milly. 'That's it, isn't it, darling? Every girl's dream. It must have been quite fabulously marvellous.'

'Yes, marvellous,' said Milly quietly.

Thorne watched her closely. He knew what the result of this kind of psychological assault could be. But Milly touched him on the arm.

'It's alright, Lance,' she said reassuringly. And then to Lady Susan. 'Well, if you really want to know how it was: I was tied up on a floor covered in chicken shit for three weeks, having to pee and everything else in front of three men who laughed and jeered and threatened to cut off my breasts. That's how romantic it was.'

However, Lady Susan was not in the least embarrassed.

'But, darling, a little suffering must have made it all the more wonderful when Lance came bursting in and took you up in his manly arms and – '

But at this point she had the belated decency to stop. She could see that Milly was getting distressed. Milly's breathing had become irregular. Indeed she was almost gasping and finally she lowered her face and put her hand to her brow. At this point Lucy Simons intervened.

'Dinner. Come on, everyone, we're going down to dinner now.'

And she herded them all out of the room. As they went down the staircase, Thorne picked up a low exchange between Dan Maitland and the girl he had brought. Dan said:

'You unspeakable bitch!'

Which naturally endeared him to Lance. Lady Susan could apparently think of nothing better to reply than: 'Oh, shut up, Dan Maitland.'

The rest of the evening was unremarkable. But that night Milly woke up again screaming. Thorne took her in his arms and held her tight. Milly moaned:

'God, she's set it off again. Now it'll go on for days.'

When Milly had calmed down sufficiently, Thorne asked:

'Why was she so mean, Milly? Where do you know her from?'

And Milly explained.

'We were at school together in Switzerland. But it wasn't that. The thing is: her father's an earl. But he worked for my father. He was our European manager. Lady Susan can't forgive me for that.'

God, reflected Thorne to himself, the whips you, people lay to your backs.

Mid-morning on the following day, Ballantyne returned from a mission to the Department of the Environment and plonked a sheaf of documents down in front of Thorne.

'Hand-outs on industrial pollution,' he explained curtly.

Thorne looked at the heap without enthusiasm.

'Nutshell, sergeant?' he requested.

'Alright,' agreed Ballantyne. 'It seems that Tyndall's Pond got its name from the haulage firm of Charles Tyndall which was prosecuted for illegal dumping and closed down five years ago. Its founder and managing director was sent to prison and the company was fined.'

Thorne was impressed. This was obviously an important discovery. The key question, however, remained.

'Fine. But is there any connection with Makepeace?'

Ballantyne nodded and Thorne detected a certain smugness lurking behind his official expression.

'Yes. In secret DOE reports. Makepeace was on holiday in Norfolk and he noticed a Tyndall lorry dumping illegally. He tipped off the police and they staked out the area.'

Thorne frowned. Something didn't add up.

'Wouldn't Nina have made the connection?'

Ballantyne shook his head.

'She probably never knew it, sir. Makepeace was told to keep it quiet for fear of reprisals from the haulage industry. Still, it seems to have got out somehow.'

Thorne drummed lightly on his desk top, a habit of his when he was keyed up.

'So the hysterical voice on the tape could have been Tyndall's wife. But, sergeant, she called Makepeace a murderer? Why?'

'Perhaps, sir,' returned the sergeant, and this time the triumph in his tone was unmistakable, 'because Tyndall hanged himself in Parkhurst two years ago.'

10

'I'm going now,' shouted John Field.

He was standing in the hall at the bottom of the stairs. He did not know which room his wife was in. For the last hour he had been packing and making preparations for his trip to Norfolk. After a moment Grace emerged from the small play-room.

'What have you been doing in there?' John asked.

'Checking Evey's work book,' said Grace. 'Her spelling's alright but her handwriting is terrible.'

John never failed to be amazed by the fierce devotion with which Grace monitored Evey's scholastic progress.

'Where is she?' he asked. 'I wanted to say good-bye.'

Grace did not answer him. Instead, with an anxious look, she asked:

'John, this won't be dangerous, will it?'

He smiled and shook his head dismissively.

'Good Lord, no. What gave you that idea?'

Beneath his buoyant manner, however, he was less confident. He was, after all, going in search of someone who might be implicated in organizing violent demonstrations. In these demos a gatekeeper had already been fatally injured and several others had been wounded. There was no evidence that the death had been deliberate. The man had been caught up in a rush of demonstrators, local people protesting at the siting of a chemical works too near to a school, and had struck his head fatally in a fall. Nevertheless, if

John was right, there were also sinister figures amongst the demonstrators and the man he was going in search of, this mysterious Nathaniel Mustard, was probably connected with them in some way.

'Evey?' John called, glancing quickly into the living room, but his little daughter was not there either. He shrugged and spoke to Grace again. 'Looks like you'll have to say good-bye for me, darling,'

He headed for the front door, Grace accompanying him. His car was parked immediately outside. It was a comfortable executive BMW. Still chatting with Grace, he pulled open the car door and immediately fell silent. He pressed his finger to his lips and pointed. Grace peeped over his shoulder. Just visible in the back of the car was a small backside. John pulled open the rear door of the car.

'Come on then,' he said with mock impatience. 'I'm in a hurry.'

Evey slowly unfurled.

'But I want to come with you, daddy,' she begged.

Grace said to her.

'Daddy's not going on a pleasure trip, Evey.'

The child said pathetically, 'It would be a pleasure trip for me.'

John was touched by this. He swung her up in his arms and hugged her.

'Oh, darling,' he said, 'I am sorry. We'll do something nice together soon.'

'But,' said Evey, 'I see so little of you.'

And John realized that she was really being a character in a soap opera, and made a mental resolution to monitor her television viewing more closely. But, for the present, he contented himself with saying: 'We'll try to do better in future. Good-bye, darling.'

He kissed her and Grace as well. Then he slipped

into the car. He started the engine and, with a wave, he rolled out of the yard and headed for Norfolk.

A quarter of an hour later he ran into what the radio told him was a three-mile tailback on the orbital. After he'd cleared that he soon found himself travelling in single file along the one open lane of the M11. This lasted fifteen miles. Motorways, he thought grimly, we'd make better time on cart tracks. It took him a full four hours to reach his destination, a small village called Dutney which proved to be exceptionally pretty. After that it only took him a few minutes to find the address he was looking for, which turned out to be a building quite unworthy of its setting. Number 21 Oakwood Heights, in spite of its evocative name, proved to be a dreary bungalow in an uninspiring side street lined with similar structures. But it did have one remarkable feature. Its front garden or yard (the American term seemed more appropriate to the barren stretch of concrete and ragged grass) was studded with wooden notice boards on which were stencilled what seemed to be bible texts. REPENT FOR THE HOUR OF WRATH IS HERE, John read as he approached the bungalow on foot. He frowned. Was that, in fact, a bible text? He was not a religious man, nor had he had a specially religious upbringing but no-one can grow up in England, going through the state system of education and later university, without acquiring a basic familiarity with the bible. The words he had just read seemed inauthentic. So did the next one which proclaimed the message: GOD WILL SORT OUT THE GOOD FROM THE WICKED AT THE DAY OF JUDGEMENT. John gazed hard at the tatty wooden board. The signs were, he decided, home-made in every sense.

He proceeded to the front door and rang the bell.

He waited a little while and then the door was partly opened by a pretty but simply dressed girl. She looked about nineteen. She wore no make-up and needed none. John strove, as one does on such occasions, to make a connection between her and the person he had come to see. Wife? Daughter? Mistress? Housekeeper? Servant? She seemed an unlikely candidate for any of these roles but he decided wife was the most likely even if it was hard to imagine this stunning girl married to the scrawny man he had seen in the press photographs.

'Good afternoon,' said John politely. 'Is Mr Mustard at home?'

The girl shook her head.

'Can you tell me when he will be in?'

She smiled suddenly.

'Oh yes. He'll be coming in at five for his tea.'

John nodded.

'May I inquire – are you Mrs Mustard?'

At this the girl drew back as if insulted.

'No, of course not,' she said angrily. 'I'm his house-keeper. Everyone in the village knows that.'

She had a trace of a Norfolk accent but it was not very strong.

John sighed. He didn't feel he was making much progress.

'Well, is there any way I could contact Mr Mustard before five?' he asked.

'No, I'm afraid not,' said the girl. 'He's out praying with the sick.'

John nodded appreciatively at these tidings. Then he ventured: 'Still, there can't be that many sick in such a small village.'

But the pretty housekeeper had a ready answer.

'Oh, he goes to the sick in all the villages round

85

about. He brings comfort to the dying. He's more respected round here than the vicar.'

John was baffled by these unexpected tidings. He had come to find a hired trouble-maker and seemed, instead, to be on the trail of a rustic saint.

'I see,' he said finally. 'Well, in that case, I'll – erm – I'll call back about five.'

The girl nodded briefly and shut the door.

John now had a couple of hours to spare. He was not hungry, having eaten a sandwich lunch on the road. He was however a little tired and knew that he would later have to drive more than a hundred miles back to London, presumably encountering the same kind of traffic hazards he had found on the way up. He decided that he would find a quiet spot and have a little nap in the car. It did not take him long to locate a field entrance off a country lane and there he put down his reclining seat and slept for a refreshing half-hour. John was one of those lucky people who can fall asleep almost anywhere as soon as they close their eyes. Waking up he suddenly remembered what Morrison, the chairman of Dinslow, had told him a few days before, information that he had passed on to the police. Tyndall's Pond, allegedly one of the largest chemical waste dumps in Europe, was supposed to be in the vicinity. John was a merchant banker rather than an industrialist but he was engaged in a takeover battle involving two chemical firms. All knowledge, he knew instinctively, is power and so he decided that he would take a look at Tyndall's Pond.

He drove to the nearest garage and filled his tank with petrol. The garage was an old-fashioned one with forecourt service and, while the car was being filled, John asked the young pump attendant if he could direct him to Tyndall's Pond.

The young man, who, in his dungarees and greasy shirt, looked more like a farm labourer than a mechanic, asked with interest: 'What's that then?'

Tom explained: 'It's a dump for waste products, chemicals – that sort of thing.'

A look of comprehension appeared in the other's eyes.

'Oh, you mean the stinking bog? Well you can't get in. Fence all round it. Two boys climbed in last year and nearly died from the stink. Like poison gas it is, see?'

'I see,' said John. 'So it's nearby, is it?'

The attendant shrugged.

'You go four or five miles, maybe a little more, along this road. Then you turn left until you come to a path – too small for cars it is and you have to walk.'

'How far do you have to walk?' asked John.

The attendant shook his head. 'Don't know. Never been there myself. Can't see nothing from the road.'

John nodded.

'Thanks anyway.'

The attendant looked at the figures on the pumphead.

'That'll be fourteen pounds, seventy p,' he announced.

Half an hour later, after a short drive, and a rather longer walk which had taken him a good mile and a half from the road into rolling, rather pretty country, John came to a fenced area at the end of the unmarked track he had been following. As far as he could judge, the enclosure comprised some fifteen to twenty acres. It was surrounded by a galvanized iron fence which was a good fifteen feet high. At intervals along the fence were signs reading: DANGER. CORROSIVE CHEMICALS. KEEP OUT. And indeed faint whiffs of throat-catching fumes reached him, displacing the delicate aroma of grasses and flowers. Nevertheless from the perimeter fence, nothing of the more sinister aspect of Tyndall's Pond, as John supposed the fenced area to be, could actually be seen. Even when John followed the fence for a quarter of a mile in either direction all he could observe within was a fairly dense plantation of fifteen- or twenty-foot-high shrubs just a little way from the perimeter fence. He thought he could just make out that the ground sloped downwards beyond the shrubs, but he could not be sure.

John sighed and stopped walking. He had come the best part of a mile from where he had left the approach path and so far he had seen nothing of interest and certainly not the actual chemical dump. He looked up at the top of the fence. It would not, he felt sure, be too difficult to climb; but of course he couldn't possibly do such a thing. It would never do for a city merchant banker to be found trespassing on DOE territory. John looked at his watch. It was later than he'd thought.

He decided that he would walk back to his car and then, if he had still seen nothing to detain him, which seemed probable since he'd already covered the ground in the opposite direction, he'd go and pay his call on Mr Nathaniel Mustard. It was just when he'd made the decision to abandon his object that John at last saw something of interest. It was a corpse.

He actually gave a shout of dismay and retreated a pace. Then he stood gazing at it with hammering heart. He could not see the whole of the corpse, but he realized it was probably a man since it was wearing heavy-duty wellies. The corpse's legs were protruding from under a low shrub. Just for a moment it occurred to John that he might not be dead but just having a nap. But was it conceivable that someone could be sleeping peacefully in that unwholesome place? John approached the fence again, and, feeling a trifle foolish in spite of his dismay, shouted:

'Hello? Hello there? Can you hear me?'

There was, as he'd expected, no response. He shouted again but the man never stirred. What should he do? Merchant bankers are neither soldiers nor explorers but like those two categories they must be able to come to swift decisions and implement them. John stepped back, looked up at the top of the fence, took a couple of running steps towards it and, with very little difficulty, clambered to the top. As he did so, it suddenly occurred to him that the thing might be electrified but he reached the top without receiving a shock. He swung a leg over and with the same ease clambered down the other side, dropping the last three feet or so. He came down in a crouching position, rose immediately and padded cautiously towards the supine form. He was practically on top of it when the look of anxious inquiry on his face gave way to one of disgust. He shook his head angrily. He stepped forward and kicked aside one of the two wellington boots protruding from under the bush. For that's all that was there. Whether by pure chance, or more likely as the result of a macabre practical joke, the two items of footwear had been placed so as to create the irresistible illusion of a body with its feet sticking out from under the low-lying bushes.

John took the other boot and flung it away. Then, just to make absolutely certain, he crouched down and peered under the apron of branches. Nothing. He had come to the rescue of a pair of discarded wellies. He glanced back at the perimeter fence. Now that the deed had been done and the trespass accomplished he thought: well, why not go on a bit? He walked a little way parallel to the interior fence but found no footpath leading into the interior. Still the shrubs were not very dense. It would be easy going. He set off towards the centre of the enclosed region and advanced cautiously. Five minutes later he came out of the shrubbery and found himself on the edge of a low bank which stretched down to a black pond. Or was it indeed liquid? It was hard to tell. It might have been a pool of tar or pitch. The surface was oily, dark and, here and there, irridescent. It looked thoroughly unhealthy and the smell which he had discerned beyond the perimeter fence was now almost overpowering. It was an acrid smell that caught in John's throat and made him cough and gasp. The pond was about the size of the average village duckpond, and there was no way of judging its depth.

John was about to turn and retrace his steps when he noticed an irregularity on the surface of the pond. Yes, there was no doubt about it. Something was either floating there or rising from the bottom of the pond. For a moment John again felt a thrill of alarm. But then he shook it off angrily. Deceived once by the illusion created by the wellies he was determined not to make a fool of himself again. He clambered three or four feet down the rather steep bank until he reached the narrow path encircling the pond. He shuddered at the thought of what his fate might be if he stumbled and fell in. Would he be consumed within minutes? Would he drown in the ordinary way or would he be able to struggle ashore – dripping treacly black substances and in need of rapid decontamination to save his life?

As he circled towards the object in the pond he reached out and grasped a short piece of broken-off branch that was lying part way up the bank. It was about two feet long and the object he was approaching seemed only about a foot from the shore. By the time John stood opposite it his faint alarm had returned. The thing did look uncannily like a body. Without further ado, John reached out and prodded it with his stick. And then, as he fell backwards a pace, he gave a cry of alarm. There could be no doubt. It was a body and it now performed a horrid manoeuvre. John realized, when he thought about the thing much later, that it must have been the density of the fluid in the pool which caused the body, after John had disturbed it, to disappear beneath the surface and then, a moment later, shoot vertically up again until it was half out of the liquid. And as it did so, John saw what was unmistakably the matted and blackened, but still recognizable, face of Nathaniel Mustard. Gasping in terror, John turned and started to scramble up the bank. Then he stopped abruptly. Standing just ahead of him, where a moment before there had been no-one, was a man.

'It's alright, Mr Field,' he said.

But it was far from alright. Thrown off balance by the new shock, John felt himself falling backwards and expected to plunge into the filthy syrup of Tyndall's Pond beside Nathaniel Mustard. Then a hand came from nowhere, took him by the arm and steadied him. A second man was next to John, and, maintaining his grip, he uttered the welcome words: 'Don't worry, sir. We're police officers.'

11

Thorne and Ballantyne followed the receptionist down a carpeted corridor at the Department of the Environment. Judging from the distance between doors, the offices were spacious indeed. It was what Thorne had expected. Mr Biscayne Mandeville was, after all, a departmental head. A computer search had turned up the name. It seemed that he had formerly worked for Messrs Charles Tyndall and Son.

Thorne had high hopes that Mr Mandeville would be able to throw light on two important questions. The first was the whereabouts of the remaining Tyndalls. There were only two of them: the widow and her son. Mrs Tyndall must be in her mid-fifties, Thorne imagined, and her son Rupert in his mid-twenties. The father, of course, had killed himself in prison. There had also been an older daughter but she had died some years before.

The second question that Thorne hoped Mr Mandeville would be able to answer was: what exactly was the nature of the link between Charles Makepeace and the Tyndalls? Thorne wanted to know how Mrs Tyndall had discovered that Makepeace had made the initial complaint about illegal dumping by Tyndall lorries.

By any rational appraisal Makepeace had not been responsible for Tyndall's death. A bell-ringing job about environmental pollution was not murder but, to a grief-stricken widow, the distinction might have seemed a fine one. It seemed conceivable to Thorne that Charles Makepeace had been killed in revenge for the suicide of Charles Tyndall in prison.

The three reached a door bearing a discreet wooden plaque upon which, in gold-edged lettering, was printed the name BISCAYNE MANDEVILLE. The receptionist knocked and a gruff voice from within called: 'Come In'. The receptionist took a step inside and said in a soft voice, 'I have Superintendent Thorne and Sergeant Ballantyne here, sir.'

'Show them in,' said the same voice.

The receptionist then stepped back and held the door open. The two detectives entered. Although policemen have to cultivate a professional impassivity, and neither man revealed his surprise, the two detectives were both aware of a distinct feeling of shock. Biscayne Mandeville was a tall and fine-looking man dressed in a good, blue, chalk-striped suit. He was also a black.

Mr Mandeville indicated two chairs on the far side of his desk. He smiled.

'Please sit down, gentlemen, and tell me what I can do for you.'

Thorne said civilly, 'Thank you for seeing us at such short notice, sir. I believe you worked for Charles Tyndall before joining the Department of the Environment?'

Biscayne Mandeville nodded.

'Yes I did.'

A trifle sternly, Thorne continued:

'Did you tell Mrs Tyndall that the information leading to her husband's arrest came originally from Mr Makepeace of Carr Sillmann?'

Mandeville leaned back smiling in his chair. He looked from one to the other. He said:

'I assume you're jesting, superintendent?'

Thorne shook his head.

'No, I'm perfectly serious, Mr Mandeville. Someone informed her and you, as deputy head of industrial pollution, were in a position to do so.'

Mandeville looked incredulous.

'And risk my job? My career? For a few hundred pounds? I take it you're suggesting I was bribed, superintendent?'

'No, not necessarily,' Thorne returned quickly. 'Mr Mandeville, I should make it clear that I cannot promise immunity but I am not at present specially interested in you or your activities. I am conducting a murder inquiry.'

This made an impression. Mandeville eased forward in his seat and frowned. He echoed softly:

'Murder?'

Thorne, watching closely, felt sure that Mandeville was not faking surprise. He continued.

'That's right. So you will understand that if you refuse to cooperate and I obtain the information from another source – '

He did not have to elaborate further. Mandeville, apparently as practised at making quick decisions as Thorne himself, said:

'I informed Mr Tyndall – not his wife.'

'I see, sir. Why?'

Mandeville sighed and then, apparently irrelevantly, offered: 'Superintendent, I have a degree in geography. And another in law.'

Thorne looked at him a trifle warily and commented: 'Very impressive, sir.'

Mandeville nodded.

'Yes. And with these impressive qualifications, the only job I was offered in three years of searching was primary school teaching. But then Mr Tyndall took me on.'

'In personnel, I believe, sir?'

Mandeville nodded again.

'Initially. But with the understanding that I would rise if I proved I was up to it. Well, he kept his word. Within a year I was head of the contracts department and when I was offered a job here he wrote me an excellent letter of recommendation.'

Thorne drew the appropriate conclusion.

'So you had cause to be grateful to him?'

'I did,' Mandeville admitted. 'I also believed what he told me.'

'Which was?' asked Thorne.

'He maintained that he was the victim of a miscarriage of justice. He insisted that his lorries had been dumping illegally because the drivers were cutting corners and not on his instructions. He asked me for the name of the man who had shopped him because he thought it might help him to mount a better defence. In the event his solicitor, as he will no doubt confirm, decided against using the information.'

'I see,' said Thorne. 'Do you happen to know of Mrs Tyndall's present whereabouts, sir?'

Mandeville looked a trifle puzzled.

'Well, of course. Blackheath.'

Thorne shook his head.

'No, she's not been there for over a year.'

A look of surprise – genuine, Thorne felt convinced – came into Mandeville's face.

'Oh? Well, in that case – '

He paused and looked thoughtful.

'Yes, sir?' prompted Thorne.

'Norfolk,' said Mandeville abruptly. 'I seem to

remember Mrs Tyndall mentioning Norfolk once or twice. I didn't know her very well, superintendent.'

'Any particular part of Norfolk, sir?' asked Thorne without much hope.

Mandeville shook his head.

'No, just Nor – wait a minute. I seem to remember her talking of the coast – the sea. That's it. The Norfolk coast. I think she spent her girlhood there.'

'She never mentioned a particular town?' asked Thorne but this time he was virtually certain that he had reached the limit of Mandeville's knowledge.

'Oh, nothing so detailed. I'm not even sure she spoke of the coast but it's an impression I have. Worth checking perhaps.'

Thorne began to rise.

'Thank you for your cooperation, sir.'

As he got to his feet, Thorne kept his eyes fixed on Mr Mandeville's face. He saw the reaction he had seen a hundred times before, a look of mingled anxiety and confusion, and he knew that in a moment Biscayne Mandeville would ask a question. Thorne got something of a thrill out of this moment which occurred quite often at interviews. When he asked himself if what he felt was a disreputable sense of power or a commendable sense of benevolence he was never quite sure of the answer.

Mandeville looked from Thorne to Ballantyne and back again. Then he asked: 'Am I likely to hear any more about this matter, superintendent?'

Thorne replied in a neutral tone:

'I can't answer that officially, sir.' He allowed a flicker of a smile to cross his face. 'But I wouldn't lose a lot of sleep over it if I were you.'

An audible sigh of relief escaped from Mr Mandeville as he leaned back in his chair. He murmured, 'I'm glad to have been of help to you gentlemen.'

And the two officers departed.

A quarter of an hour later, as Thorne and Ballantyne approached the ramp leading to the underground car park at Wood Street, a radio message started coming through.

'Stop the car,' said Thorne urgently, knowing that once they were under the overhang of the garage the radio message would be muffled if audible at all. Thorne had already heard the name John Field and he had an idea that the message might prove important.

Ballantyne promptly braked and the two men listened. They learned that the two plain-clothes officers who had, on Thorne's instructions, been following Field for days had pursued the banker up to Norfolk. There, unhappily, they had lost him for a time as a result of a burst tyre on their own car. When they had repaired the damage they had searched for and soon found John Field's car again not far from a chemical waste dump known as Tyndall's Pond. Inside the enclosure they had located John Field with the body of a man.

'Rates a chopper, wouldn't you say?' asked Thorne.

'Pity they lost him, sir,' said Ballantyne, as he slotted the car rapidly into Thorne's bay in the car-park.

'Why?' asked Thorne sharply.

'Well,' said Ballantyne dubiously, 'if they'd stayed with him they'd have caught him in the act or – '

'Exactly,' continued Thorne. 'Alibi'd him. Not John Field's lucky day, is it?'

'So you still think he's innocent, sir?'

'Yes. But he seems determined to prove me wrong. Well, let's get up to Norfolk and find out what this is all about.'

An hour later Thorne and Ballantyne were clattering through the sky above East Anglia at a temperate one hundred and twenty miles an hour. The trip lasted about an hour and a half and then the two detectives found themselves descending vertically on to a scene of great animation. Parked as close as possible to a dark, fenced pool were five or six cars and a trailer interview room. Uniformed policemen hurried about and the area had been marked out in complex ways with tape.

A few minutes later, Thorne and Ballantyne entered the mobile interview room to encounter John Field. The young banker was clearly very angry but also frightened. Thorne noticed with approval that he was concealing the latter emotion with considerable success.

'You had me followed,' said Field reproachfully as soon as he saw the London detectives.

'That's right, sir,' agreed Thorne mildly, as he seated himself opposite the suspect.

'Why?' demanded Field.

'Well,' returned Thorne, 'let's just say I judged it desirable.'

'Was it because you suspected me of murdering Charles Makepeace?'

Thorne smiled faintly.

'Would you mind greatly if I asked the questions, sir? It's the more orthodox procedure.'

Field looked disconcerted.

'Sorry. But am I under arrest, chief superintendent?' he asked.

Thorne shook his head.

'If you were, you'd have been cautioned, sir. You're helping me with my inquiries.'

'Isn't that supposed to be voluntary?'

Thorne smiled meaningfully.

'Exactly, sir.'

It only took Field a moment to realize that the superintendent was implying that Field could still be cautioned if it became necessary. He sighed.

'Alright then, superintendent,' he said. 'How can I help?'

'What did you do when you left Mustard's bungalow?'

Field shrugged and shook his head.

'I've been through it several times with the local police.'

'We'd get through it more quickly, sir, if you could just answer my questions.'

'I understand,' agreed John wearily. 'Alright, I drove for a while and then I had a short nap in the car. Then I went and bought some petrol.'

'Yes,' said Thorne. 'We've had that confirmed by the garage attendant.'

'And after that,' said Field, 'I went to Tyndall's Pond. For God's sake, your men were following me. They can confirm it.'

'I wish they could, sir,' said Thorne. 'Unfortunately they had trouble with their car and lost you.'

'So,' said John, 'your theory is that I came here looking for Mustard, found him and killed him with my bare hands and then hoisted him over a twenty foot fence and dumped him in that bog.'

But Thorne was not moved by the irony. He merely commented mildly: 'Someone seems to have done just that, sir.'

Field looked at him incredulously.

'But no man could have done it alone.'

'Oh yes, he could, sir,' returned Thorne, 'if he was reasonably fit and knew the right technique.'

Field gazed at him in dismay.

'You mean, superintendent, that you seriously think that I – '

But Thorne cut him off.

'No, I don't, sir. But at this stage what I think isn't important. After all, you've admitted that you came here looking for Mustard.'

'But not to kill him. I wanted to talk to him.'

'Very likely, sir.'

Thorne looked at him wearily.

'Look, am I going to be charged, superintendent?' he asked plaintively.

Thorne shook his head.

'No, sir. In fact, you're free to go.'

Field leaned back in his chair with a sigh of relief.

'Thank God for that,' he exclaimed.

'But,' warned Thorne, 'until we find out who did kill Mr Mustard, we may want to interview you again. Will you be going straight back to London?'

Field nodded.

'Well, take care how you drive,' said Thorne soberly. 'You've had a bad shock. There could be a delayed reaction.'

12

The next morning, Ballantyne entered Thorne's office in a state of mild excitement.

'Carl Senner and Micky Baylis,' he announced. 'Do those names mean anything to you, sir?'

Thorne thought for a moment and then ventured: 'South London gangsters?'

'That's right,' said Ballantyne, impressed, as he often was, by his chief's memory. 'Well they smashed themselves up yesterday in their Mercedes. One dead and the other just hanging on in intensive care. They crashed through a barrier on the M25 and flattened the Merc against the bridge support. They'd just come off the M11.'

'Being chased, were they?' asked Thorne.

Ballantyne shook his head.

'No, sir. But they both had phenomenally high blood alcohol levels.'

'So? Two hoodlums on a drunken spree. Why should we care?'

'Because, sir,' said Ballantyne, 'Micky Baylis had a scrap of paper in his wallet with an address on it.'

Thorne was getting a little impatient.

'Alright – whose address was it?'

'Nathaniel Mustard's sir,' said Ballantyne triumphantly.

Thorne put down his ball-point and leaned back in his chair. He understood the implications at once.

'And they were coming down the M11 – from Norfolk – '

'Well, we can't be sure – '

'From Norfolk,' repeated Thorne firmly. 'Where they'd stabbed Mustard to death and dumped him in Tyndall's Pond.'

'Oh? Do we know that he was stabbed, sir?' asked Ballantyne.

Thorne pushed a pathologist's report towards him.

'Came through this morning. He was dead before he hit the swamp. No fluid in his lungs. Maybe those two boneheads thought Tyndall's Pond was full of some kind of acid and would dispose of the body for them. But it's more likely they'd have wanted people to know what happened to Mustard.'

'You're ahead of me, sir,' said Ballantyne with a slight frown.

Thorne eyed him reflectively.

'Any evidence apart from the address?' he asked.

'Yes, but needs confirmation. Traces of what was probably Mustard's clothing in the boot. Mud that probably came from the Norfolk site on the tyres. Other bits and pieces. So why do you think they killed him, sir?'

'Probably as an example. I think he hired them to whip up the demos at the Dinslow plants and then failed to stump up their fee. He probably sent it to Christian missions or something like that. He was a religious nut but he was also a fairly shrewd operator. He should have known you can't mess about with psychopaths like Micky Baylis. Interesting to know for sure why they dumped him in that place.'

'Good chance that Baylis will pull through, sir. So perhaps he'll tell us in due course. Seems to put Field in the clear, doesn't it?'

Thorne nodded.

'More important, it wraps up the Mustard killing

and more or less proves it was unrelated to the Makepeace one. Of course we still can't completely eliminate Field as a suspect for that. What we need now, sergeant, is some new leads.'

The very next day, one turned up.

Two ladies, one in her sixties and one in her eighties, entered Hampstead police station. The younger of the two told the sergeant on duty that the other lady, her mother, had actually witnessed the break-in at the Makepeace cottage.

Since all the houses in the neighbourhood had been visited by police at the time and all local residents questioned, the sergeant naturally asked why it had taken her so long to come forward. It turned out that the old lady had been visiting her daughter but had returned to her home in the country before the search had started. It had never occurred to the younger woman that her mother might have seen anything. But it so happened that on the relevant night, the old lady had not been able, after retiring early, to sleep. She had risen from her bed and gone to the window of the room. This overlooked the square and so provided a good view of the cottage. The old lady had seen a person on foot approach the Makepeace home, glance about cautiously and then slip along the narrow passage beside the garage, climb over the wall and disappear from view. Soon afterwards she had returned to her bed, had fallen asleep and had forgotten all about the incident until she had again visited her daughter and learned of the police inquiries.

The old woman's evidence was, of course, important. It provided the first independent confirmation of Isobel Makepeace's story. Previously her assertion that there had been a break-in, although compatible with certain signs discovered at the site, had been unsupported.

Thorne and Ballantyne went up to Hampstead to visit the old lady. There, in a small house on the opposite side of the square from the Makepeace cottage, they were shown the window from which the intruder had been observed. The window did indeed command an excellent view of the Makepeace home. But the old lady proved to be a trifle vague. Although Thorne spoke to her gently and patiently he was able to obtain little of interest beyond what she had already told the police. The one thing he did find out was far from welcome. When speaking of the intruder the old lady referred to whoever it had been as 'she' rather than 'he'. Thorne had refrained from challenging this unexpected pronoun until he had finished questioning her. Then he asked her if the intruder had been a woman. The old lady shook her head vaguely and said:

'I don't really know.'

Thorne pointed out that she had regularly used a feminine pronoun but the old lady did not seem to understand.

'Yes,' she said cooperatively. 'I suppose it could have been a woman.'

'Could it have been a man?' asked Thorne.

'Oh, indeed yes, constable,' she returned, demoting Thorne drastically.

As he and Ballantyne drove away from the Hampstead square, Thorne felt distinctly unhappy about the new development. Of course, the old woman had undoubtedly been vague and prone to error. Her eyes, as her daughter had made clear, were none too good even with glasses. The distance across the square was considerable and it had been evening. And yet she had spontaneously used feminine pronouns. Why? Because she had actually seen a woman or just imagined it had been a woman because of some chance impression conveyed perhaps by clothing designed to deceive? Thorne hoped that she had not really seen a woman. He disliked arresting women for murder. Indeed he disliked arresting them at all.

In his youth, Thorne had been taught by his mother always to be chivalrous towards 'the weaker sex'. She had stressed to him that women were physically frailer than men and that therefore they must be treated with courtesy and protected if necessary. She had, for example, insisted that young Lancelot Thorne should stand up and give his seat to women in buses and trains.

Brooding about the old lady's account that evening at home, while Milly, prone on the floor, drew up lists of furnishings for the new country cottage, Thorne realized that it was probably his mother's early training which had led him to acquire Milly in the first place. It had been his innate chivalry, as much as anything, that had led him to attempt to find her when she had been kidnapped on Corsica.

Shortly after his appointment as superintendent, Thorne had spent a short holiday on the island. He had originally planned to go there with a girl-friend but she had been compelled to call off the trip at the last moment. Thorne had gone alone. While he was on the island a sensational kidnapping had occurred. A young American heiress had been taken from the villa in which she had been holidaying with her family. Soon the family began to receive ransom notes. Thorne, who had been successful in locating a kidnap victim during his tour of duty in Bristol, had offered his services to the local carabinieri. His offer had been treated coolly at first. After all the English detective spoke very little Italian and did not know the territory. But, after telexes had been exchanged with London, Thorne had been invited to pursue discreet investigations.

He had volunteered because he had read many accounts of the experiences of kidnap victims in Corsica and Sardinia and was haunted by thoughts of the nightmare the rich and spoiled young American girl must be experiencing. He also felt that he might succeed where the locals had failed and, moreover, succeed precisely because he was not a local. He devised a technique of investigation in which his lack of Italian could be a positive advantage. It was very simple. Armed with a photograph of the victim, Millicent Cardington, whose father was the largest manufacturer and distributor of alcoholic drinks in America, he drove about the island showing it in cafés and shops. He claimed to be the kidnapped girl's brother from America, and he restricted himself to saying, in barely understandable Italian: 'My sister – have you seen?' Naturally, he was unable to understand most of what he was told in reply but then he was not much interested in words. He was interested in the little signs that tell more than words. He knew that the small peasant communities on Corsica were very clannish. He believed that people living in the area where the girl was being held would know something. They would not be criminals. They would not have any precise knowledge. But they would be aware that she was nearby. This knowledge they might very well be able to disguise when questioned by local police but, Thorne reasoned, they might inadvertently disclose it to an assumed relative. And he proved to be right.

It took Thorne nearly three weeks of combing the remote places. He had obtained an extension of his leave from the City commissioner but towards the end of his investigation he began receiving telexes urging him to return.

In most of the villages into which he drove in his big American Lincoln, people did their best to help, examined his photo closely, speculated, talked it over with each other, shook their heads, made suggestions – in other words behaved as you'd expect. But at last he came to a village where his production of the photo produced only shakes of the head, silences, covert glances. Thorne realized at once that his search was over.

He informed the carabinieri that, in his opinion, the girl was being held somewhere in the surrounding hills. Discreet but intensive observation was initiated and, within a few days, a suspect who had come into the village for provisions was tracked back to a smallholding in the foothills where photographic proof was obtained that someone was being kept in a shed in the field behind the main house.

Thorne was with the party which stormed the place the next day. They had found Milly: emaciated, terrified and filthy but physically unmolested. Four Corsican shepherds had been arrested after a short gunfight which was noisy but harmed nobody. Following their trial the four received life sentences. The rescue made headlines in England, Corsica and America just as, three months later, the announcement of an engagement between the victim and the young English police officer who had found her also made headlines.

'Lance,' said Milly, intruding on his musing, 'do you like Persians?'

Reluctant to abandon his train of thought Thorne merely murmured:

'They're called Iranians now, I think.'

'No, I mean Persian carpets,' said Milly irritably.

'I've bought three but I'm worried they won't be delivered in time for our house-warming. Lance, should we invite the commissioner?'

This preposterous suggestion had the effect of breaking Thorne's concentration. He looked at her astounded.

'Sir Basil? To a party given by a chief superintendent?'

Milly looked defiant.

'Well, why the hell not, Lance? I bet it'll be the best party old Commissioner Plod's ever been to.'

Thorne gazed at her in amazement. He was about to remonstrate some more when Milly glanced at the clock on the mantel and jumped to her feet.

'Hell,' she exclaimed. 'I promised the Bannisters we'd look in for a drink after dinner. Come on, we're late as it is.'

13

The most important breakthrough in the investigation so far was undoubtedly the location of the Tyndalls. Ever since Biscayne Mandeville had mentioned Norfolk as a county he associated with Mrs Tyndall, the Norfolk police had been searching for her. On Friday afternoon, they found her. The widow of the late Charles Tyndall, who had hanged himself in Parkhurst, was living in a wooden-framed house amongst the dunes a stone's throw from the sea and near the village of Hemsby. Also inhabiting the house was her son, Rupert, who had once been his father's junior partner. Rupert, the police discovered, now worked in a foundry that manufactured wrought iron. Mother and son, had, it seemed, befriended a local girl who did a certain amount of housework for them.

Thorne, when notified of the find, had been very insistent that the local force must under no account let the Tyndalls know that they were under suspicion. He wanted to get their unprepared reactions to the hate-tape from Carr Sillmann. Nevertheless he ordered that their seaside house should be put under surveillance. He didn't want these two prime suspects suddenly taking fright and disappearing again as they had from London.

He instructed Ballantyne to make all necessary arrangements for a visit to Norfolk. He wanted a police car and the use of an interview room in the most suitable local police station. The next day he and Ballantyne took the train to Norwich. Thinking things over on the train Thorne realized that all the evidence pointed to Mrs Tyndall. A woman's voice, presumably hers, was on the tape. The old lady in Hampstead thought she had seen a woman breaking into the Makepeace cottage on the night when, it was assumed, the poison had been put into Charles Makepeace's flask. Thorne sighed. He hated violating his chivalrous instincts by arresting a woman but if it had to be done he wouldn't hesitate.

At about noon he and Ballantyne, in their borrowed police car, approached the low, whitewashed frame house, separated by a few reedy dunes from the beach, in which the Tyndalls were allegedly living. Just out of sight of the house they came upon an unmarked police car in which a young man sat munching a sandwich and reading a paper. Thorne stopped and spoke to him. He learned that Rupert Tyndall had gone to work as usual that morning and that Mrs Tyndall was still in the house. She did not appear to go out much.

'And he works in a foundry, is that right?' asked Thorne.

'Yes, sir,' said the young constable. 'It's about a mile back along this road – right in the village. Used to be the Hall. Now it's run as a business. They make wrought-iron work – stuff like that. Rupert's the foreman.'

Thorne thanked the surveillance man and then he and Ballantyne continued on to the dusty yard outside the front door of the house. They got out of their car, walked the few steps to the front door and rang the bell. It was soon opened by a pretty girl who looked as if she might be about eighteen. This was the daughter of a local greengrocer who spent a good deal of time at the Tyndalls. The local police thought that she was probably Rupert's girl-friend.

Thorne smiled and said politely:

'Good afternoon, we're police officers. Are you Ellen?'

'That's right,' said the girl looking surprised. She had a Norfolk accent.

'Would you please ask Mrs Tyndall if we could have a word with her?' Thorne requested.

'Alright,' she agreed.

Whereupon she started to shut the door on them. Thorne said quickly but pleasantly:

'Perhaps we could come in and wait?'

From Ellen's reply he gathered that the girl was no friend of the police.

'No, you couldn't,' she snapped tartly. 'Not till I find out if she wants to see you.'

With which she closed the door firmly in their faces. Happily the wait was only a short one and then the door opened again and Ellen said: 'She'll see you – this way.'

She led them along a short passage and then through a door into a surprisingly spacious living room in which there were six living things. Five of them were cats, four kittens and their mother all in the same basket. The sixth was an erect, shrewd-looking lady in advanced middle age who was seated in an upright chair that had padded arms. The chair looked, in fact, like a good piece of furniture. With a quick glance round, Thorne confirmed that much of the rest of the furniture in the room, including a grand piano and a sideboard, also looked as if it had once graced a much more imposing house.

The woman looked at them very composedly as Ellen pulled the door shut behind them.

'I understand you're police officers,' she remarked

in crisp upper-class tones that nevertheless betrayed a hint of a Norfolk accent.

'That's right, madam,' replied Thorne. 'Detective Superintendent Thorne and Sergeant Ballantyne, City of London Police.'

The lady nodded.

'Detectives – I see. Well, I really can't think why detectives should be interested in me.'

'I'll be happy to explain,' Thorne assured her. 'But first, are you Mrs Allison Tyndall, widow of the late Charles Tyndall of Messrs Charles Tyndall and Son?'

Mrs Tyndall drew back her head in what Thorne was convinced was merely the pretence of surprise.

'Yes, that's right,' she agreed. 'You know all about me. How amazing.'

Thorne smiled inwardly. He realized that this lady, frail as she looked, had a strong will.

'Do you have a son, a Mr Rupert Tyndall?'

'Yes, I do,' replied Mrs Tyndall. 'He's at work.'

'Of course,' said Thorne quietly. Then, very abruptly and in a considerably louder voice, he demanded: 'What can you tell me about the death of Mr Charles Makepeace?'

She was clearly nonplussed. Thorne inferred this from the way her eyes narrowed briefly. But she gave nothing else away.

'Who did you say?' she asked.

'Mr Charles Makepeace,' repeated Thorne.

'Yes, of course. I'm trying to remember. He was the junior minister that was sacked last week, wasn't he?'

Again Thorne smiled inwardly and this time even a trifle exultantly. He often enjoyed his work but never more so that when engaged in a mental struggle with a resourceful opponent. He said quietly:

'Charles Makepeace was an executive with the merchant bank of Carr Sillmann. He was murdered ten days ago.'

'I am sorry to hear it,' said Mrs Tyndall.

'Are you?' asked Thorne. 'I find that a little surprising. You see, Mr Makepeace supplied the evidence which ultimately led to your husband being imprisoned.'

'Are you quite sure?' asked Mrs Tyndall and there was a hint of satisfaction in her voice as if, like Thorne, she too obtained pleasure from the exchange.

'You didn't know that?' asked Thorne.

'Certainly not,' replied Mrs Tyndall.

'Well, that's very strange – because a Mr Biscayne Mandeville of the Department of the Environment, has admitted passing the information to your husband.'

'Has he really?' replied Mrs Tyndall. But Thorne felt that she now realized that the sands beneath her feet were beginning to shift.

'So you've never heard of Mr Mandeville?' he attempted.

'Yes, I have,' she admitted at once. 'I've just remembered. There was a Mr Mandeville – yes, that's it, Biscayne Mandeville – who worked for us – that is, my husband.'

Thorne said, a trifle pointedly:

'And have you also remembered that Mr Makepeace was the person who informed on your husband?'

Mrs Tyndall nodded and said, a trifle wearily: 'Yes, I've remembered that too now. I suppose I deliberately suppressed the unhappy memory. You see we've built a new life here. It's where I spent my childhood.'

Thorne leaned towards her to deliver the crunch question but, as he did so, he accidentally tapped the kitten basket with his foot.

'Do be careful!' snapped Mrs Tyndall as a faint squeal arose from the squirming animals.

She reached down and patted the kittens protectively. The mother cat licked her hand. Mrs Tyndall took up one of the kittens which she placed in her lap. She gently stroked it as the conversation continued.

'I'm very sorry,' apologized Thorne. 'But now I have to ask you, Mrs Tyndall. Why did you make abusive phone calls to Mr Makepeace?'

A look of the most perfect astonishment came over Mrs Tyndall's face. She even smiled, as if from the intensity of her surprise.

'What, superintendent? What are you talking about?'

In spite of his irritation, Thorne again found himself admiring her self-possession.

'I'm talking about threats shouted down the telephone,' he amplified.

'I know nothing about them,' averred Mrs Tyndall.

Thorne leaned back in his chair. He looked sideways towards Ballantyne and, when their eyes met, he made the slightest of nods. It was a signal for Ballantyne to take up the interrogation. There were two reasons why Thorne wanted this. In the first place, Thorne was not the kind of officer who treated his sergeants as mere assistants or even adornments to enhance his own rank and power. His last sergeant was now a chief inspector with the Metropolitan Police, a high-flyer who was proving to be almost as impressive as Thorne himself had been. But Ballantyne, of all the sergeants Thorne had worked with, struck him as the most promising. It was time for him to try his wings in a difficult interrogation. Also, of course, a switch of interrogator often had a disorientating and therefore valuable effect on the suspect.

Ballantyne slipped smoothly into his role.

'May I ask, Mrs Tyndall,' he began. 'Didn't you feel angry about what Mr Makepeace had done?'

The woman drew back her head slightly, as if to put the younger man in his place.

'Sergeant,' she proclaimed impressively, 'My son and I have suffered. Suffering burns out anger.'

'So,' said Ballantyne, 'you deny that you ever shouted threats on the telephone?'

'I hardly ever raise my voice, sergeant.'

'I think I should tell you,' said Ballantyne, apparently diffidently, but, Thorne noted with approval, actually reducing the suspect's space for manoeuvre, 'we have a tape recording of a woman making such threats.'

Mrs Tyndall shook her head positively.

'That's of no concern to me, sergeant.'

'Perhaps you weren't aware,' went on Ballantyne, 'that Mr Makepeace recorded your threatening calls.'

Thorne wondered if possibly Ballantyne might be being a little too direct. But before he had time to think much more about the matter his concentration was disturbed by the sound of a motor cycle approaching the house. He turned slightly in his seat to look out of the window that gave on to the yard and, as he did so, accidently gave the basket containing the kittens a sharp kick with his foot. This time the squeals were louder. Mrs Tyndall, who had doubtless been readying herself to deny that she had ever shouted threats down the telephone now gave the game away.

'You fool! You clumsy fool! How dare you?' she screamed.

Thorne and Ballantyne exchanged an exultant glance. What they had just heard was undoubtedly the same hysterical voice as that on the tape. Thorne got to his feet immediately.

'Mrs Tyndall,' he said formally, 'I must ask you to answer some specific questions in connection with the murder of Mr Charles Makepeace.'

He then began to utter the statutory caution which so many policemen think gives criminals an unfair advantage.

'You are not obliged to say anything but I must warn you that anything you do say – '

And at this point there was a dramatic interruption. The room door burst open and a tall, well-built young man took two steps into the room. His fists were clenched and his arms were raised slightly. Thorne realized at once that this could be none other than Rupert Tyndall. He also guessed why Rupert Tyndall was there. Doubtless Ellen had, on her own initiative, gone to the foundry to fetch him. And doubtless it had been the sound of his motor cycle which they had heard a moment before.

At this new development a note of fear came into Mrs Tyndall's voice. She gripped the arms of her chair and gazed in dismay at her menacing son.

'Rupert,' she exclaimed. 'Control yourself! Do you hear me? Sit down at once!'

But the young man paid no attention to her. He took another step towards Thorne who was glad to note, from the corners of his eyes, that Ballantyne was on his feet too. This was clearly a powerful young man but the two of them should be able to handle him.

In the tones of Oxbridge, which rather surprised Thorne, issuing as they did from what was apparently the heavily muscled body of a labourer, Rupert Tyndall said:

'You're making a fool of yourself.'

'Oh?' asked Thorne quietly. 'In what way?'

In reply, Rupert Tyndall turned on his heels and left the room. But not for long. A moment later he returned, preceded by a flying wheelchair that Thorne only just managed to side-step before it came to rest against a chair.

Rupert snarled: 'My mother can't walk. She had a stroke after father's death.'

Thorne felt a surge of relief. The old woman in Hampstead had been wrong. She had not seen a woman break into the Makepeace cottage. She had seen a powerful young man. Something he had been wearing, or something in her own mind, had made her think of a woman. But now Thorne knew that he would not have to violate his chivalrous instincts. Mrs Tyndall had undoubtedly made the threatening phone calls. But she had not been able to act on her threats. Her son had been the agent of her revenge. Thorne turned to Rupert Tyndall.

'In that case, sir,' he said formally, 'perhaps I should ask you the questions I was going to put to your mother – about the murder of Mr Charles Makepeace.'

At this Mrs Tyndall, in spite of her condition, managed to push herself half way to her feet as she cried:

'No! Rupert was here with me – the whole time! The whole time!'

14

Thorne sat in his living room turning through the transcriptions of his many interrogations of Rupert Tyndall. Milly lay on the floor in front of the open fireplace reading *The Tatler*.

'Cunning bastard,' remarked Thorne.

'Rupert Tyndall?' asked Milly wearily.

Police officers were not supposed to discuss their work at home but most of them did. Thorne was no exception and Milly usually enjoyed sharing his cases with him. But by now she had begun to feel that she had had enough of the Makepeace murder. Thorne had been almost visibly crackling with nerves for the past week.

'He's getting away with it,' grumbled Thorne. 'I've leaned on him as hard as I can and he won't confess.'

'Well, can't you forget him?' suggested Milly. 'And get on with the next case?'

'For God's sake, Milly,' expostulated Thorne. 'It's not a tough question in an exam. It's murder.'

'But, Lance, why are you so sure he's guilty?'

'I'm not, but he's the best suspect I've got. And there's a good deal of circumstantial evidence.'

Milly got up from the floor and sat down on a comfortable chair opposite her husband.

'Alright then,' she suggested. 'Give me a run-down. Who is he exactly?'

'He's the son of a man that committed suicide in prison. He has no valid alibi for the night the poison was put in Makepeace's flask. He swears he was making love to Ellen, the girl who acts as his mother's housekeeper. She confirms this but then she's clearly besotted with him and totally unreliable. Now I'm convinced that he murdered Makepeace because he considers him responsible for his father's death. His vindictive and unbalanced mother put him up to it.'

'And where does this delightful family live, Lance?'

'In a little town called Hemsby in Norfolk. Rupert works in a place that makes wrought iron.'

Milly looked interested.

'Hell, Lance, I've been looking for a wrought-iron supplier. We need some for the party. Why don't I pop up to Norfolk and buy some from your murderer?' She laughed lightly. 'Maybe I could get him to confess at the same time?'

Thorne gazed at her narrowly.

'Don't even joke about it,' he warned her. 'I could get drummed out of the police for less.'

Milly shrugged.

'Okay, okay,' she protested. 'Only trying to help.'

Later, Thorne wondered if there had been something in his manner which had contradicted, or which might have seemed to Milly to contradict, his warning. God knows, he had needed a little help. He had questioned Rupert Tyndall non-stop for three days. He had played him the tape of his mother's scream of abuse on the telephone. It had rattled Rupert alright but he had admitted nothing. Thorne was convinced that he had his hands on the murderer of Charles Makepeace but he hadn't a single piece of evidence other than the tape. There was no way he could get Rupert Tyndall into court without a confession. So was it possible that he really had asked Milly to help him? Not in words, of course. In words, he had told her quite properly and correctly that any interference in an investigation

119

by a relative of a police officer would bring down strong disciplinary action on that officer. But had he, by his manner, his anxiety, his neurotic harping on the case, even the selective details he had confided in her, really been asking her to take a hand? Because that's exactly what she did. Thorne didn't know about it at the time, of course. If he had done, he would have had to stop her.

The very next day Milly drove in her Jaguar to Hemsby. She had no difficulty in finding the large house on the outskirts of the little market town which had been converted into a foundry and showroom for wrought-iron work. For some time, she wandered about the showroom, examining the tables and benches and intricate fencing turned out by the craftsmen employed on the premises. Before long, she was approached by a young woman sales assistant and, after negotiation, Milly ordered a substantial quantity of wrought iron. Then she asked about 'someone called Rupert' pretending she couldn't remember the last name. She said a friend of hers had bought several items and that this Rupert had advised her about installation.

The young woman explained that Rupert was the manager, but that he was out on a delivery that afternoon. Milly seemed quite distressed by this and managed to convey to the saleswoman that if she couldn't have Rupert's advice she might have second thoughts about the goods she'd ordered. In the end she achieved her objective. The young woman gave her Rupert's home address.

When, a little later, Milly drove into the dusty yard in front of the Tyndall home, she immediately saw Mrs Tyndall. The incapacitated lady was seated under a small wooden sun-shelter by the side of the house. Milly parked her car, got out and went towards her. As soon as she was close enough, Mrs Tyndall called:

'Can I help you?'

Milly smiled and advanced a little closer.

'I hope so,' she said. 'I'm Milly Cardington. I've come from the foundry. They told me that Rupert Tyndall would be here.'

Mrs Tyndall frowned slightly.

'Well, he's gone to the chemist for me, I'm afraid. I'm his mother.'

Milly smiled enthusiastically.

'Really?' she asked. 'A friend of mine bought some wrought iron off him. She said he knew everything there was to know about it. I just wanted to consult him.'

'I see,' nodded Mrs Tyndall. 'Well, if you'd care to wait.'

For the next half hour Milly sat and chatted with Mrs Tyndall. The truth was that she liked the old lady immediately and, before long, she began to feel that the response was reciprocated. They were both intelligent upper-class women, interested in the same kind of things. Their minds worked alike. Milly was an American who, before her marriage, had lived a fast, international jet-setting life. Mrs Tyndall had lived more sedately. Nevertheless the two women shared many attitudes.

After a pause in the conversation, Mrs Tyndall peered back along the dusty road, which bore little traffic since it only led to the dunes and the Tyndall house.

'I can't think what's keeping Rupert,' she remarked. 'Of course they run out of my pills at the local chemist's

121

sometimes. If that's happened, he'll have had to go into Yarmouth.'

Milly frowned slightly.

'Yarmouth's a long way, isn't it?' she inquired.

'I'm afraid so,' Mrs Tyndall agreed. 'But Rupert's so good about these things. Why do you know he – '

But she never completed the remark. Milly felt a little pulse of frustration. She felt sure that Mrs Tyndall had been on the point of saying something indiscreet. Instead the older woman pulled herself together and suggested: 'It's getting a bit chilly. Why don't we go indoors and have a cup of tea?'

Milly said, trying to maintain the air of just having called casually:

'Well, I wouldn't want to outstay my welcome.'

Mrs Tyndall immediately protested.

'Oh, but it's a pleasure having you. We get so few visitors. When we lived in London we led a very full social life but since my poor husband – '

Once again she checked herself. Then she went on: 'Do come in, my dear, and you can help me to make the tea.'

'Well, if you're really sure,' said Milly, looking very doubtful.

'Quite sure. I haven't enjoyed an afternoon so much for ages. Would you mind pushing me, my dear?'

Milly immediately stood up and grasped the handles of the wheelchair. Although unable to leave the chair Mrs Tyndall nevertheless managed to make tea and toast very competently and the two women had an agreeable tea party. But at the end of it Milly began to doubt if she would learn anything that might be of value to Lance. She glanced at her watch. It was getting late. There was no sign of Rupert. Perhaps he had returned to the foundry. At this thought, Milly remembered the other reason for her visit. She had bought some rather fine pieces of ironwork but she had forgotten the tree guards for the young Japanese cherry trees which must be protected from the party guests who would be jostling on the lawn. She decided to call again at the foundry on her way home.

'That was very nice,' she said politely. 'But I guess I shouldn't stay any longer. I have to go by the foundry again to get – '

At this point Milly had an inspiration. It came from her knowledge of the crime and its antecedents. She knew that Charles Tyndall had died in Maidstone Prison with a rope made from strips of prison clothing round his neck. Even as these facts passed swiftly through her mind she heard herself saying:

'So I was wondering if perhaps your husband could help me?'

Mrs Tyndall frowned slightly. But that was the only sign of discomposure she gave.

'Husband?' she returned.

Milly nodded. 'Well, yes, Rupert's father – he owns the foundry, doesn't he?'

Mrs Tyndall shook her head slowly.

'No, I fear he doesn't. As a matter of fact, he's dead. He committed suicide six years ago.'

Afterwards Milly was surprised at how easy it had been. She had never done any acting even in school plays and yet she had fallen effortlessly and, judging from the result, convincingly into the role of sympathetic comforter.

'Suicide!' she exclaimed. 'Gee, that's terrible!'

Mrs Tyndall nodded grimly.

'Oh, we've had troubles, Miss Cardington. You wouldn't believe the half of it – and it still continues. Can you imagine this? Someone who was an enemy of our family, who was, in fact, responsible for my husband's death, has been murdered.'

At this Milly gasped as if in horror and echoed: 'Murdered?'

Mrs Tyndall leaned forward confidentially. And as she did so Milly guessed that she, Milly, had done what she had set out to do. From now on she would be able to manipulate the older woman.

'Yes,' said Mrs Tyndall, 'but that's not all. The police are trying to prove a case against Rupert.'

'Case?' asked Milly, as if bewildered. 'What kind of case?'

Then she drew in her breath sharply and said in a hushed voice: 'You're not saying – you don't mean – the police think your son is a murderer?'

Mrs Tyndall smiled. She seemed suddenly very calm and relaxed.

'Yes, they do,' she said almost cheerfully. 'But what they don't understand is that it wasn't murder at all. It was simple justice. You see Makepeace as good as killed my husband and so Rupert – hang on, I think that's him now.'

As a roar from Rupert's motor cycle reached them from the beach road it suddenly seemed to Milly like an excellent time to be on her way. But at precisely that moment her new-found acting talent deserted her. She told Lance afterwards that she sat with her mind racing, trying to think of some plausible reason for making a sudden departure. But none occurred to her. She was just toying with the idea of simply getting to her feet and bolting when the door opened and a tall, physically impressive young man entered. As soon as he saw Milly he stopped dead and said, 'Oh,' softly. Mrs Tyndall smiled and Milly noticed that her arms spread slightly as if to embrace her son.

'Rupert!' she exclaimed, 'You were a long time.'

Rupert smiled faintly.

'Sorry, mother, I had to go into Yarmouth.'

Mrs Tyndall immediately offered Milly a meaningful look as if to say: isn't he a good and thoughtful son? Then she turned back to Rupert.

'I'm so sorry, dear. I told Miss – '

Then she frowned. She had, for the moment, forgotten Milly's last name. She looked appealingly at her guest. And now Milly made a terrible blunder. Even as she said the fatal word she realized that she'd given herself away.

She smiled brightly at Rupert Tyndall and said: 'Thorne. It's Milly Thorne.'

It took Mrs Tyndall a moment or two to react. Then she said:

'Really? But I thought – '

Milly tried hopelessly to retrieve the situation.

'Cardington. Sorry, don't know why I said that. It's Milly Cardington.'

There was what seemed like a long silence although really it only lasted a few seconds. Then Rupert made the connection.

He shook his head slowly.

'You said "Thorne".' He looked at his mother and added, 'Superintendent Thorne is the name of that policeman.'

Then Mrs Tyndall, in a voice from which all trace of her former cordiality had vanished, looked at Milly and said:

'You're not connected with Superintendent Thorne, are you, my dear? Yes, I see you're wearing a wedding ring. Is it possible that you're his wife?' And now her voice hardened into menace. 'Have you come here on police business, Mrs Thorne?'

Milly was now, as she later reported to Lance, genuinely frightened. She was alone in a lonely house with a woman who had recently as good as admitted to her that her son was a murderer. And that son, an impressively powerful young man, was gazing at her without a trace of warmth. In spite of her instinctive sense that it was an incriminating thing to do, Milly found herself taking a few steps backwards.

'Me?' she said, trying to pass it off. 'Do I look like a cop? I'm just here to buy some wrought iron.' She turned with a false smile to the young man. 'You see, Rupert, the thing is, this friend of mine – well she bought some iron from you – and she said you were the biggest expert she ever met – so I thought maybe you'd help me to – you know help me – well – '

The other two gazed at her in stony silence and finally it overwhelmed her. She too fell silent. Milly wondered what would happen next and, fleetingly, whether she would be able to stay ahead of Rupert if it came to a chase. Then Mrs Tyndall broke the silence in an unexpected way.

'Go, Rupert,' she urged. 'You know where. There'll be more of them here before long.'

Rupert sighed and turned towards the chair-bound woman.

'But, mother – '

'Don't argue!' hissed Mrs Tyndall. 'They could be watching the house. Just go.'

Rupert said no more but moved towards the door. As he did so, he kept his eyes fixed on Milly. He had to pass within inches of her. She braced herself. Would he seize her by the wrists? Would he attempt to take her hostage? Would he throw a punch as he passed? But with no more than a dark look of contempt, he strode out of the room leaving the two women, who

126

were now enemies, to gaze without speaking at each other until they heard the roar of his motor cycle.

Then Milly began to back slowly towards the door. She found she was keeping her eyes fixed on Mrs Tyndall as if to prevent the crippled woman from springing at her. No word was exchanged as Milly felt behind her for the door handle, found it and then turned and flung herself out of the house. She found herself running as if from the devil. And as she ran she gasped and moaned in terror. She knew that it was not merely the ordeal she had just been through which was affecting her. It was also the echo which any danger always set up, the echo of her Corsican nightmare. She should never have come to this dreary house on the dunes. She had done no good. She had obtained no evidence. Oh, it was clear that Rupert was the murderer but Thorne had already known that. And how would he react when he found out about her meddling?

Milly reached her car. As she pulled the door release she paused. Echoing across the dunes came the stutter of a motor cycle engine. Milly gave a brief cry of alarm. It must be Rupert returning. She scrambled into the car but when she went to insert the ignition key into its lock she found her hands were trembling so much that she could barely manage it. And the motor cycle was getting louder. Finally, she succeeded in slotting the key home. As she started first the engine and then, almost immediately, the car itself, a motor bike came round the bend of the beach road. It was not Rupert's bike and there were two people on it. Milly gave a violent shudder of relief and then, engaging gear, shot away from the sea and the Tyndalls.

15

Milly sat at her desk in her study with a ball-point pen in her hand and a small note-book in front of her. She had written at the top of the first page of the note-book: CHECK LIST FOR PARTY. These words were underlined. She had completed the heading a good half an hour ago and yet there was nothing else on the page. Try as she might Milly could not keep her mind on the party. Instead she kept thinking about the front door.

A few minutes later she heard it open and, almost immediately, close again. At the sound Milly rose from her desk and went to the door of her study. But, as she heard Lance's feet on the stair, she turned, rushed back to her desk and pretended to be writing. As he passed her door, doubtless on his way to their bedroom in order to change into casual clothes for the evening, she called out:

'Lance?'

There was a slight pause and then the door opened and her husband entered. He stood at the door gazing at her impassively. He said nothing at all.

She swallowed and said: 'Well?'

He sighed. He knew what she wanted to know. Finally he said: 'I was rebuked.'

Then he turned as if to depart. Milly said quickly, 'Hey, man, I'm sorry. Is that very bad?'

He turned back. Then, after another short pause, and to her great relief, he sat down on the brocaded sofa opposite her desk. He smiled wryly.

'It's better than being hung.'

She swallowed.

'So you're still a copper? You haven't been slung out or anything?'

He shook his head.

'No, I'm still a superintendent.' But a hard note entered his voice as he added: 'But because of your meddling, Milly, I'm likely to remain one for longer than I would have done.'

Milly looked horrified.

'Is that what he said?'

'No,' said Lance, 'that is not what the assistant commissioner said. That is not how it's done in England. He was very sympathetic and said it was rotten luck and could happen to anyone. But what he really meant was that I'm an unreliable laughing-stock who can't even control his own wife, never mind the villains.'

Milly returned a shade defiantly: 'I can't see what I did that's so very terrible.'

'Well, let me clarify it,' said Thorne softly. 'You interfered with an investigation and as a result a murderer is on the run.'

'But Lance,' she expostulated, 'I told you. I only went there to try and get some wrought iron.'

Thorne didn't raise his voice.

'You went there to play detective,' he said.

'No, I – ' began Milly but then she stopped, abruptly having decided that candour probably would be her best course.

'Okay,' she resumed, 'so maybe I did think that if I could get a confession out of the old woman it would help you.'

In an almost conspiratorial voice, Lance said: 'If the assistant commissioner suspected you'd gone there for any other purpose than the wrought iron, I'd be back on the beat.'

'Well, he won't suspect. Lance, have you got a lead on where Tyndall's hiding? Are you going to catch him again?'

'We're looking,' said Thorne soberly. 'But we haven't got any leads.'

'But, Lance,' said Milly with a sigh. 'I told you. She knows. The old woman – Mrs Tyndall – knows where he is. I'm certain of that.'

'It's possible,' said Thorne with a shrug. 'But she won't admit it. I've interviewed her twice.'

'Have you told her I know? Have you challenged her with that?'

'With what exactly?'

'Lance, I heard her say to Rupert: you know where to go. Tell her I heard it. See what she says.'

'Alright. The next time I interview her.'

'When will that be?'

'Possibly tomorrow. Depends if anything more urgent comes up – like getting a lead on Rupert.'

But by ten o'clock the next morning, there were no reports on the missing suspect and Thorne decided to pay another visit to the house on the dunes. He had not, in fact, tackled Mrs Tyndall with what Milly had heard her say and he was not sure why. His normal practice with suspects or witnesses was more like that of a psychiatrist than an interrogator. He gave them their head. He let them meander if they wanted. He tried to fathom what they really meant even if they weren't sure themselves. He had once seen, in his days as a DC, a veteran chief inspector question a witness with such brutal urgency that the witness actually forgot evidence that she wanted to impart and which would have spared the police a long and difficult investigation. Thorne had decided then that it was best to let whatever was in a witness's mind emerge at its own rate. Nonetheless he should have confronted Mrs Tyndall with what Milly had heard. It would probably have triggered some kind of reaction and all reactions were messages if only you could interpret them.

Thorne was half way to Liverpool Street Station, which was no distance from Wood Street, when the phone rang. The WPC who was driving him answered it and said: 'It's for you, sir. Sergeant Ballantyne.'

Thorne took the call, wondering, with a faint spurt of excitement, if Rupert Tyndall had been spotted somewhere. But the message did not concern Rupert. Ballantyne told him that he had just had a call from another suspect, the astrologer, Musquat Singh. It seemed that Singh had returned from his conference in America and, learning that the police had made inquiries about him, had phoned to announce that he was available for interview.

'What do you think, sir?' asked Ballantyne, when he had relayed this intelligence. 'Do you want to postpone your trip to Norwich?'

Thorne glanced at his watch. He could allow himself a couple of hours for Singh and still get an afternoon train that would get him to Norfolk in time to see Mrs Tyndall. Thorne was, moreover, curious to meet the great astrologer who was, he knew, many times a millionaire and who was retained not only by Carr Sillmann but by a variety of other important organizations and individuals.

'What did you tell him?' Thorne asked Ballantyne as the WPC filtered the car into the approach road to Liverpool Street Station.

'Thanked him for calling. Told him we'd be in touch.'

131

'Not necessarily today?'

'No, sir.'

'In that case, perhaps it would be a good idea to pay him a flying visit. Try and catch him on the hop.'

'So you don't want him notified that we're coming?'

'No. Meet me there, outside the house. Oh, where is the house by the way? I haven't got the address with me.'

'Twenty-four Lady Lane. It's a narrow street that connects West Heath Road with Chalmers Avenue – a bit like a country road if I remember right.'

'There may be a driveway. Meet me out of sight of the house. Understood, sergeant?'

'Yes, sir.'

Thorne hung up and apologetically said to the WPC, who was just easing them to a halt in the entrance bay of the station, 'Sorry, constable, change of plans. Can you take me to Lady Lane in Highgate?'

Lady Lane proved to be, as Ballantyne had suggested, very reminiscent of a country road. It rose steeply, with few houses visible and most of these large mansions set well back from the road and surrounded by sizable gardens. There were no pavements but the lane, barely wide enough for two-way traffic, was flanked by young trees, lawn and shrubbery.

About half a mile from the lane's entrance, they came upon Ballantyne sitting at the wheel of his Rover. Thorne thanked the WPC who had brought him and then went to Ballantyne's car. The sergeant got out respectfully.

'This the house?' asked Thorne, looking at a substantial villa, in the manner of a Tuscan farmhouse, set some way back from the road.

Ballantyne shook his head with a faint smile. He

pointed to an entrance drive, framed by a wrought-iron gate, that led into a dense tangle of rhododendron and swamp oak.

'Good Lord,' Thorne exclaimed. 'Could lead to a great country house.'

A few minutes later, their car issued from the wooded area to curve round a large croquet lawn and up to the entrance of a noble Victorian mansion that, Thorne decided, could not have contained fewer than twenty rooms.

They left their car on a gravel forecourt and mounted a short flight of stone steps to the ornate front door, surmounted by a large brass zodiac. They rang the bell and before long it was answered by a tall and smiling Indian boy of about eighteen. He was dressed in a turban, green silk knee breeches and a gorgeous flowered shirt. Thorne was no authority on national costumes but he felt the outfit owed less to India than to Hollywood.

When they gave their names, the boy grinned broadly and said, in a flawless Cockney accent:

'Come on in. The master's expecting you. My name's Ali.'

Thorne and Ballantyne exchanged an amused look and then followed the lad through a large hall decorated with a variety of oriental and astrological motifs into an even more colourful drawing room.

'I'll tell the master you're here,' said the young Indian and then left.

'Do you think, sir – ' began Ballantyne, only to break off abruptly as Thorne pressed his finger to his lips.

Ballantyne realized that his chief was telling him that an ingenious astrologer might well have hidden mikes in his visitors' reception room.

133

'I think,' said Thorne pointedly, 'I'll catch the afternoon train. But I won't need you, sergeant. You can do some paper-work while I'm gone.'

'Right you are, sir,' said Ballantyne.

And then the two officers were silent for the three or four minutes that passed before the door opened and a plump, smiling little Indian, dressed in a light-weight, blue suit, entered.

'Welcome, gentlemen,' he said, beaming, 'to my rather extravagant home. Ali is making you some fresh coffee.'

'There is no need,' said Thorne politely.

'There is great need,' Singh contradicted civilly. 'Hospitality is a sacred obligation. I believe you are here on official business, chief superintendent?'

'That is correct, sir,' said Thorne formally. 'And Ali has told us that we're expected. Exactly why are we expected, sir?'

Musquat Singh smiled and seated himself in an astonishing armchair which was shaped like a baby elephant.

'I wasn't expecting you at this moment,' he said. 'But I have been in contact with the bank and learned that you have inquired after me.'

'In that case, sir,' said Thorne in an official tone of voice, 'you will know that we are investigating the murder of Charles Makepeace.'

Singh nodded quite cheerfully.

'And I'm a suspect because I disliked the drunken old bore. Is that it, superintendent?'

Thorne smiled inwardly. That was a clever stroke. He had intended to reserve his knowledge that there had been animosity between the two men for a strategic moment. But the astrologer had deftly undermined the stratagem.

'Perhaps you could tell me, sir,' Thorne resumed, 'what you were doing on the night of the 8th of June?'

This did surprise Singh. He frowned. He shrugged his shoulders. He looked puzzled. Finally, he repeated: 'The 8th of June? But that was not the date on which Charles Makepeace died.'

'Just answer my question, please, sir,' said Thorne with a touch of severity.

Singh removed from the inside pocket of his jacket a small diary and turned through it for a moment.

'Well, let's see,' he murmured. Then he found the place.

What he read there apparently caused him to hesitate for a minute before continuing: 'Oh – yes – the 8th of June – well, as it happens, superintendent, I did nothing. On that night, I stayed at home.'

It was not true, or not the whole truth, felt Thorne. 'Can anyone confirm that?' he asked.

'I'm afraid not,' said Singh smoothly. 'It was Ali's day off. I was in my room alone, working. And in the event he did not show up.'

'Who did not show up?' asked Thorne quickly.

Singh seemed a little flustered.

'Well – a person phoned. You know, superintendent, they often phone me. Asking for an appointment. Wanting to pick my brains. I said I would give him ten minutes. But he never showed up.'

'And who was this person?' asked Thorne. 'May I have his name, please?'

'I'm afraid not,' said Singh apologetically. 'You see?'

He held out his diary for Thorne's inspection.

'I only wrote an initial "M".' He laughed. 'There must be quite a few "M"s in London.'

'In that case perhaps you could – ' began Thorne but fell silent when there was a knock at the door.

'Come in,' called Singh immediately, almost as if grateful for the diversion.

Ali entered with coffee and cups on a tray.

'Leave it, Ali,' said Singh.

'Yes, sir,' said Ali.

He carried the tray to a small ornamental table. Thorne resumed his interrogation.

'So in fact you saw no-one at all on the evening of the 8th of June?' he asked the astrologer.

Thorne uttered the words 'the 8th of June' loudly and clearly. He wanted Ali to hear them.

Singh smiled deprecatingly.

'I'm afraid not, superintendent. I have no alibi.' He laughed again. 'So I hope you have brought your handcuffs.'

And at this point Ali took the bait. The young Indian, who had been on his way back to the door, paused. Then he turned and said:

'The 8th of June? Hang on, master. That was my girl-friend's birthday. I can give you an alibi.'

Thorne immediately addressed Ali.

'Now what's your girl-friend's birthday got to do with it?'

Ali grinned conspiratorially.

'Went to see her, didn't I?' he said. 'We was going out for eats. But she had 'flu. So I come home early.'

He looked at Musquat Singh and appealed to him.

'Don't you remember, master? I brought you some tea about ten.'

Singh waved his hands feebly in the air.

'Really?' he said. 'I had forgotten.'

'That's right,' continued Ali. 'And I remember that when I got in – abaht 8 that was – you was 'aving an argy with some geezer.'

'Be quiet!' ordered Singh sharply.

Ali looked puzzled.

'But if you need an alibi – '

'I need obedience,' snapped Singh. 'So be quiet and get us some more coffee.'

The young Indian shrugged and departed.

Thorne deliberately refrained from taxing Singh with Ali's remarks and the rest of the interview was quite straightforward.

When Thorne and Ballantyne were back in their car and heading once more for the railway station so that Thorne could resume his interrupted journey to Norfolk, Ballantyne asked:

'Which one is telling the truth, sir?'

Thorne smiled.

'Which do you think?' he asked.

Ballantyne said:

'I think they both are.'

Thorne contented himself with mildly requesting, 'Explain.'

'They've got their dates muddled.'

'Wrong,' said Thorne positively. 'Ali is telling the truth and the astrologer is lying.'

'How do you know, sir?' asked Ballantyne curiously.

Unapologetically, Thorne said: 'Instinct. And until you develop it, sergeant, you'll never make inspector.'

It was Ballantyne's turn to make a telling point: 'Instinct cuts no ice in court, sir.'

Thorne sighed.

'Which is why we poor jacks get ulcers,' he said wryly.

There was a pause. The gothic towers of St Pancras came into sight. Ballantyne asked cautiously, 'So why is Musquat Singh lying?'

Thorne shrugged and said quietly, 'Perhaps his visitor – the one that Ali heard – was a professional hit man.'

Ballantyne was surprised by this lurid suggestion.

'You really believe that, sir?'

Thorne said: 'I don't need to *believe* anything at this stage, sergeant. It'll do as a working hypothesis. You'd better wait a few days and then go back and question Ali again.'

'Me, sir?' asked Ballantyne, surprised.

'You, sergeant. You're closer to his generation. Talk to him about pop groups, things like that. Get matey. Find out all the things Ali's forgotten that he remembers.'

Ballantyne smiled.

'Right you are, sir,' he said.

16

Thorne slept in the train. He dreamt that he was being presented to the Queen. The trouble was he wasn't absolutely sure why. He had an idea that it might have been because of some splendid piece of detective work that he'd pulled off. He had, after all, been officially informed that the Queen was going to present him with the WDM – the Wonderful Detective Medal. But the crowds lining the route to the palace, along which he was being driven in an immense limousine with horse-guards prancing beside it, were not cheering. Instead they seemed disgruntled. He noticed that they kept pointing at him and whispering. He thought to himself: I'm only getting the medal because of Milly.

And that's all Thorne could remember of the dream when he woke up. But he was astonished, as often before, at the vivid detail. He could, by turning his mind to the appropriate scene, describe with professional accuracy the appearances of several of the people in the crowd. He could see the glistening flanks of the horse nearest to his window. The dream had also contained bizarre and surreal elements. The limousine had been roofed with a kind of castle keep and Thorne had several times glanced anxiously at trees ahead and worried that they might be hit by the high turret. But even the weird elements of his dream were visually clear to him after awakening.

Some years before Thorne had read a number of volumes of the works of Sigmund Freud with deep fascination and, on the whole, belief. But Thorne did not need to resort to the theories of Freud to interpret his dream. He was pretty sure that he would have been able to reach a fairly accurate understanding of it even if he had never heard of the great Viennese doctor. It was not so much an inferiority as an insecurity dream. Thorne had had the dream, or variants of it, quite often and he was persuaded that it expressed something he was never consciously aware of when awake: a sense of social and professional insecurity. Could anything be done about it? Not, he felt, while he remained married to Milly. Because the hard fact was that his wife came from a world that had given her a confidence, and a network of acquaintances, that he would never match even if he did, in the end, become 'top cop'. And it was the contrast between their backgrounds which generated his dreams. So what was his best course? Leave Milly? He smiled at the notion as he watched the wooded and hilly countryside apparently slide past the windows of the intercity express. He couldn't leave Milly. He needed her too much. Not for her money or her contacts or her devotion. He needed her for her sheer, unquenchable vitality.

It was late in the afternoon when Thorne finally reached the Tyndall home amongst the dunes. He was admitted as usual by Ellen who seemed no longer hostile to him but merely indifferent. She left him just inside the front door, went away and returned in a few minutes to nod and lead him to her mistress. Thorne followed the girl into the living room, with its view of dunes and the distant white foam of breaking waves.

Mrs Tyndall was seated at her davenport writing a letter. She looked up as Thorne entered.

'Good afternoon, superintendent, I expected you this morning,' she remarked.

'Unavoidable delay, I'm afraid,' returned Thorne

briefly. He approached her. 'I see you're writing a letter.'

She made no attempt to conceal the text.

'That's right,' she acknowledged. 'Not to Rupert, of course. I'll stop now. Ellen,' she addressed the girl who was waiting silently by the door. 'Help me to the other chair, would you?'

'Allow me – ' began Thorne, but Mrs Tyndall instantly silenced him.

'No thank you, superintendent. Ellen can manage.'

A few minutes later they were seated opposite each other, while Ellen went off to make tea. Thorne reflected on how very English and, indeed, slightly dotty, it was for him to be taking tea with the mother of the murderer he hoped to put behind bars. Mrs Tyndall interrupted his reflections with: 'You haven't found him, have you, superintendent?'

Thorne smiled.

'Why do you say that, madam?'

Mrs Tyndall waved the question away with the remark:

'Clearly you wouldn't be here if you had.'

'You know,' said Thorne earnestly, 'it would be better for everyone, and that includes Rupert, if he were found.'

'Really?' asked Mrs Tyndall, her voice thick with scepticism. 'In what way?'

Thorne did not mince words.

'He could kill again.'

Mrs Tyndall was not dismayed. She shook her head firmly.

'Rupert's no murderer,' she said quietly. 'But even if he had – had executed the man responsible for my husband's death, he would still be no threat to any other living soul.'

141

'In terms of statistics, that's simply not true,' said Thorne. 'Murderers frequently murder again, if only to escape capture. It would be much better if he were safe in custody.'

Mrs Tyndall smiled in a faintly superior way.

'Then you'll have to find him, won't you, superintendent?'

'There is an alternative,' said Thorne.

'Oh? What?'

'You could tell me where he's hiding.'

'What makes you think I know?'

'My wife heard you say to your son: "You know where to go".'

Mrs Tyndall shook her head and smiled.

'Oh, all I meant by that was that Rupert would find some suitable place. Now then, I suppose you want to search the house, do you?'

'Not this time,' said Thorne.

Mrs Tyndall did not seem surprised.

'No, you know he's not here, don't you? You have a man watching the house. We take him a glass of lemonade sometimes. It must be miserable sitting in that little car.'

For want of anything better to do, Thorne rose and crossed to the large window overlooking the dunes. He could just see the nose of the constable's mini. He frowned. It shouldn't be visible. Not that it seemed to matter much in the present case. Thorne turned back to the room and began to move towards his seat again. But something attracted his attention. He knew this room quite well by now. He had often noticed the photograph before but never studied it closely. It stood on a small, circular table by itself. Thorne walked to it and picked it up. As he looked at the attractive, but perhaps a trifle severe-looking, young woman it portrayed, he realized, even as Mrs Tyndall spoke, who it must be.

'Beautiful, isn't she?' asked the old lady and there was great sadness in her voice.

Of course, it must be the dead daughter, Margaret.

'Your daughter, I believe?' said Thorne sympathetically.

'Oh, come, come, superintendent,' the tone of the old woman's voice had changed to one of irritation. 'You know all about us. You know that Margaret died of a heart thing – a rotten rheumatic illness that is so rare no-one in England knew how to treat it – when she was only thirty-two.'

'She was a writer, I believe?' Thorne said, ignoring the bitterness.

As he said this, he turned instinctively to the bookcase, which held perhaps a hundred volumes, that stood behind the table. He ran his eyes along the titles and, with a faint shock of surprise, he saw the name Margaret Tyndall on one of them.

'She was an architectural historian,' Mrs Tyndall said. 'She wrote a splendid book on English ruins. She was enormously talented. She would have written many more books only the silly girl had to go and die.'

Thorne removed from the shelves a large-format illustrated book. He began to turn through the pages, noting splendid black-and-white photographs of ruined buildings.

'Looks very interesting,' he murmured. 'My wife is an enthusiast – '

He was cut short by Mrs Tyndall saying angrily:

'Did I give you permission to touch my books, superintendent?'

Thorne was surprised.

'No, but I – '

143

'Then kindly replace it.'

Thorne did so.

In a somewhat less hostile voice Mrs Tyndall continued, 'I only have that copy. And very little else of Margaret's. And now, if you have no further business with me today, I should like to get on with my letter.'

Thorne, although he strove not to show it, had been angered by her peremptory manner.

'May I just remind you – ' he began in an official tone of voice. But she once more seized the initiative.

'Yes, yes, superintendent, I know. I have committed a felony by helping a suspect to escape. I am only at liberty because of the remarkable benevolence of the police. But unless you intend to carry me away in irons would you please leave now.'

And notwithstanding the professional detachment he cultivated and quite often achieved, Thorne realized that he was seething with impotent anger as he rose, nodded politely and left the room. It was only when he was driving away from the house that he smiled ruefully and murmured under his breath, 'And I didn't even get my cup of tea.'

At about mid-morning on the following day, Ballantyne entered Thorne's office and placed on his desk an illustrated book entitled 'Important English Ruins.' Thorne nodded in satisfaction.

'Good. Was it hard to get hold of?'

'Not really,' said Ballantyne. 'The publishers had loads of them left – remaindered they call it. Seems they only sold a few. But they said she would have had a great future if she'd lived. They think the photographs are first-rate.'

'She took them herself, didn't she?' asked Thorne.

'Oh, yes,' said Ballantyne. 'Wrote it and photographed it. That book represents three years of fieldwork. Tell me, sir: why are we interested?'

Thorne shook his head.

'I'm not sure. Something about Mrs Tyndall's manner when I handled it. She pretended to be angry, but I had an idea she was really afraid. Attractive girl,' he added thoughtfully, contemplating the frontispiece which showed Margaret Tyndall in front of Fountain's Abbey in Yorkshire. Behind the girl, whose severe safari outfit and short hair could not conceal her beauty, was the large caravan which doubtless served as her base for fieldwork. Thorne turned idly through the book until he came to a splendid photograph of a ruined castle. The building, crowning a low hill, rose from a sea of mixed woodland. It was clearly very isolated.

'What do you think, sergeant?' he asked Ballantyne, holding the book so that his sergeant could see the picture. 'Make a good hide-out?'

'Could be,' Ballantyne nodded. 'But don't ruins have caretakers?'

'Do they?' asked Thorne. 'You'd better find out. My guess is you'll find some do and some don't. Naturally what I want is a list of those that don't.'

'Take some time, sir.'

'Tell you what. Get that girl, Betty, in admin, the bright one, to help you. She can do the basic dogsbody and you can do the final listing.'

'Well – ' said Ballantyne, and glanced at his watch.

'What's the matter, got a date?' asked Thorne irritably. He was not a martinet but he did have a fondness for seeing his subordinates move when he told them to do something.

'As a matter of fact, yes, sir. With Ali. Remember?'

Thorne sighed. His sergeant had a bad habit of being a jump ahead of him.

'Alright,' he said grudgingly. 'Flit up to Highgate. I'll have a word with Betty myself. But I want a comprehensive report on the ruins by tomorrow lunch-time, alright?'

Half an hour later, Ballantyne, alone in the car, turned into the gates of Musquat Singh's mansion in Highgate.

As his car rolled to a stop outside the front door Ali himself appeared from around the side of the house. It was clear to Ballantyne that the youth had been waiting there for his arrival. Ballantyne got out of his car and Ali approached him.

'Sorry to have wasted your time,' he said with a somewhat hangdog look. 'I called you but you'd already left.'

Ballantyne knew, of course, that Ali had called. The message had been telephoned through to him. And it had naturally only increased his interest in what the young Indian might be able to tell him.

'Something wrong?' asked Ballantyne, watching the other closely.

Ali shook his head with an attempt at a carefree smile.

'No, nothing at all. It's just that I got it all screwed up. I only remembered a little while ago.'

'Remembered what, exactly,' asked Ballantyne.

'Different night, wasn't it? You know, the night I come 'ome and 'eard my master with someone.'

'But that's impossible,' said Ballantyne politely. 'Don't you remember? It was your girl-friend's birthday?'

'Right, right, so it was,' Ali agreed. 'And I did go

146

round to see 'er and I did leave early. But what I forgot was that I went to the pictures after I left her.'

'Oh, the pictures?' repeated Ballantyne, po-faced.

'Right,' said Ali firmly. 'Down in Islington. Saw "Beth the Virgin" – very avant-garde film. You seen it?'

Ballantyne ignored the question.

'So, are you telling me,' he probed, 'that you didn't get home until late?'

'That's right,' said Ali. 'Pretty late – abaht ten thirty.'

'And so you didn't hear your master, Musquat Singh, with someone?'

'On the button,' said Ali.

'I see,' said Ballantyne, nodding thoughtfully. 'There is just one thing I'd like to know.'

'What's that?' asked Ali.

'Why are you lying?' asked Ballantyne.

But Ali was not put out. He smiled grimly.

'Out of line, sergeant,' he said. 'Any old how, 'fraid I can't stop and chat. Got to chop garlic. But if I do remember anything, I'll give you a buzz.'

He turned on his heels and went back the way he had come. Ballantyne looked after him with a reproachful shake of his head. For a moment he felt an impulse to go up to the ornate front door and ring the bell. He wanted to tell Musquat Singh that his fancy servant was telling lies to the police. But, of course, it would probably be Ali that opened the door. For that reason, Ballantyne decided, it might be best to use the radio-phone in the car. That way he could call the astrologer direct. But Ballantyne knew that his urge to do so stemmed essentially from anger, and he also knew that an angry policeman is a bad policeman. Sighing, Ballantyne got back into his car, started it, drove down the quarter-mile-long drive and out into Lady Lane. Then he phoned through to Wood Street to consult his chief. But Thorne, as it happened, had just gone upstairs to see the assistant commissioner. Ballantyne decided against waiting in the vicinity. He drove back to Wood Street.

Later that afternoon, in Thorne's office, he asked: 'Do you think Ali's been got at, sir?'

'With a bulldozer,' Thorne said firmly. 'Driven by Musquat Singh. But why? What's Singh trying to hide?'

'What you said?' suggested Ballantyne. 'Hiring a hit man?'

Thorne nodded.

'Begins to look like it. Trouble is I still think Rupert's our boy. Anyway, we'd better follow Ali around a bit and see what he gets up to. Take care of it, would you, sergeant?'

Ballantyne arranged for surveillance on Ali.

The next three days were intensely depressing. The two detectives now had a brace of suspects but no activity on either front. A DC in plain clothes followed Ali everywhere but the young Indian's daily round seemed innocence itself. Thorne was not too concerned about Ali's lack of incriminating behaviour, since he still held firmly to his conviction that Rupert Tyndall was the guilty man. He still hoped that, in Margaret Tyndall's beautifully illustrated book of ruins, he held the key to Rupert's hide-out. But by the end of the week every single ruin in the book had been investigated. Some that were close to London had been visited by Thorne and Ballantyne. At one of them, the remnants of a lovely moated grange deep in Surrey woodland, they had found two runaway school-boys living in a tent high in a turret. Similar discoveries were being made by local police all over the country

who flushed out many tramps and winos, a few deca-
dents hopefully practising black arts, any number of
illicit lovers, but no Rupert Tyndall.

On Friday morning, Thorne sat moodily at breakfast
turning the pages of Margaret Tyndall's book. Then
he sighed, snapped it shut and prepared to leave for
the city.

'What are you doing?' asked Milly.

Thorne looked at her in surprise.

'I'm going to work, Milly. I always do at this time of
day. You must have noticed.'

'But it's Friday, Lance,' she said plaintively.

'What of it?' he returned.

'Our party!'

'Our party's tomorrow, isn't it?'

'Oh, Lance,' she reproached him. 'Have you forgotten? You said you'd help me today. There's a million
things to do.'

He gazed at her in astonishment. Was she suggesting
that he take the day off? And then he remembered.
That was exactly what she *had* asked him to do. It had
been about a week ago. And he had agreed without
giving it much thought, or rather thinking that he'd be
able to wriggle out of it when the time came. But he'd
forgotten about it and now she'd be furious if he let
her down. Well, what was waiting for him on his desk?
A hundred things, naturally, but the blunt truth was
that until there was some breakthrough – either in
finding Rupert Tyndall or, as regards the long-shot, in
getting more evidence against Musquat Singh – there
was not much concerning the Charles Makepeace
investigation that couldn't be left to Ballantyne for the
day. And he knew how Milly had toiled to get the
house ready for the party.

He sighed.

'I'll have to make a phone call,' he said briefly.

He made the phone call and arranged for Ballantyne to hold the fort. And then, a little later, he and Milly drove out to the Queen Anne mansion that was already busy with party preparations. Electricians were hanging fairy lights from the trees. Carpenters were laying an outdoor dance-floor. Caterers were bringing in food and drink. It was, Thorne had to admit, a rather delightful scene. As they sat in Milly's Jaguar contemplating it, he put his arm round her and leaned down and kissed her on the ear.

'You done good, baby,' he murmured.

She smiled gratefully.

Just after he and Milly finished unrolling an Ispahan carpet in the small living room. Thorne stood up and gazed around. The room now looked splendid: elegant but not austere, rich but not forbidding. He wiped his brow. It was a glorious, and very hot, summer day.

'Sit down for a minute, Lance,' suggested Milly. 'I'll get us a couple of lagers from the kitchen.'

'Thanks, darling,' he said. 'but let's have them on the porch. It'll be cooler there.'

She nodded and hurried away. Thorne went out of the drawing room into the great stone-flagged hall where a team of electricians was engaged in installing strobes and lasers for the next night's celebrations. He continued on through the hall and out on to the columned porch, beyond which was the gravelled drive and then the great lawn stretching away to a grove of birch saplings. Thorne sat down on the steps. In his shirt-sleeves he looked like one of the many workmen about the place.

Before very long, he heard the crunch of tyres on gravel and looking to his left he saw a saloon car drawing a large caravan approaching. It swung round the drive and stopped in front of him. From the driver's seat of the car an attractive young woman got out and spoke to Thorne who had, by this time, risen to his feet and was gazing hard at her.

'Hi,' she called. 'I'm Anna Williams, Catering supervisor. Where can I park this rig?'

And she jerked her head sideways to indicate her caravan. But Thorne did not answer her. Instead, with what looked like unbelievable rudeness, he turned and strode into the house. Anna Williams stared after him in affronted amazement. But Thorne hadn't been rude. He had simply been overtaken by a revelation. And the revelation had been of such tremendous importance that the instant it had appeared he had forgotten the girl who, inadvertently, had been responsible for it.

Thorne knew only that he needed to get to a telephone. That was why he had hurried away from Anna Williams to where the nearest one was located, on the octagonal table in the ground-floor hall. He dialled and, a very short time later, he was talking to Ballantyne.

'The caravan, sergeant,' said Thorne urgently.

'What? Is that you, sir?'

'It is – Thorne. The caravan, that's where he is.' Ballantyne was quick-witted but the abruptness of the message defeated him.

'I'm sorry, sir?' he said anxiously.

'We're thick, sergeant, both of us. Rupert Tyndall – he's in the caravan.'

'I see, sir. Which caravan exactly?'

'Margaret Tyndall's. That's why Mrs Tyndall took fright. He's not holed up in a ruin but in that caravan.'

'Makes sense, sir. Where is the caravan?'

'I haven't a clue. So I'd be grateful if you'd find it and let me know. You've got one hour.'

'One hour!' came the appalled voice of Ballantyne.

'Okay, one and a half. Ring me back the moment you know.'

And Thorne hung up.

He stood for a moment in thought. Then he remembered the girl who had driven up with the caravan and his unintentional rudeness. He hurried back out on to the porch. Milly was there with two open cans of lager but the girl and her caravan were nowhere to be seen.

17

'That must be them, sir,' said Ballantyne, pointing ahead to where a police car stood at the entrance to a narrow lane on their left. It was late afternoon, less than five hours since Thorne had phoned Ballantyne and instructed him to trace Margaret Tyndall's caravan.

In that time, a great deal had been accomplished by integrated police work. A second copy of Margaret Tyndall's book had been obtained from the publishers. The make and model of the caravan had been identified. The manufacturing company had been contacted. Computer records had been searched. The date of the caravan's sale to Margaret Tyndall and its registration number had been established. Department of Transport records had been combed to establish the caravan's last known location. When all this had been done the divisional police had been notified and they had soon established that a young man corresponding to Rupert Tyndall's description was living in the caravan. They had been instructed to keep watch on the caravan and to await the arrival of Superintendent Thorne and Sergeant Ballantyne of the City police. And now, less than five hours after Thorne's flash of inspiration, the trap was closing.

'The same county,' Thorne marvelled, as Ballantyne pulled up near the waiting police car. 'We've been searching England for him and he's practically been a neighbour.'

As their car drew to a halt the door to the marked police car opened and a uniformed inspector got out.

Thorne and Ballantyne left their own vehicle and Thorne approached the Inspector.

'Inspector Mallory?' he asked politely.

'That's right, sir,' said the other. 'You've made good time.'

Thorne nodded.

'Is chummy at home?' he asked.

'Oh yes,' the inspector assured him. 'I've got a constable keeping an eye on him. Up there.'

He pointed to where a small figure was just visible beside a hedgerow about a quarter of a mile away on a low hill. The inspector raised his arm and the distant constable raised his in apparent acknowledgement.

'Has he got a radio?' asked Thorne.

The inspector shook his head.

'No. We thought it better to keep radio silence, sir. Can't be sure what chummy's kitted out with.'

'Right,' said Thorne. 'Well, you know the lie of the land. You and your men had better do the cross-country stuff. We'll approach up the lane here. How far is it?'

'Just over a mile to the field entrance,' said the inspector. 'Seems longer because it's so narrow.'

'And you're quite sure there's no other approach?'

The inspector shook his head.

'Only the fields. And they're pretty tough going. If he tried escaping that way we'd easily cut him off.'

Thorne nodded.

'Well, he's a big lad, but we should be able to hold him.'

The inspector and three men, leaving the driver in the car, entered the field on either side of the road and began to move towards an invisible location. Thorne and Ballantyne climbed back into their car and began to drive very slowly down the lane. Their speed was dictated by two factors. One was the necessity to synchronize their arrival with that of the police on foot. The second was the fact that the lane was so narrow that the plants on its steep banks brushed the car on both sides and thus restricted it pretty much to walking speed. In this way they crawled for about half a mile, at which point Thorne exclaimed angrily:

'What the hell – '

Ahead of them on the road stood a uniformed constable. Ballantyne stopped the car immediately in front of the man and the two London officers waited for the constable to squeeze between the bank and the car to reach Thorne's window.

'Weren't you the one watching the caravan?' asked Thorne sternly.

The constable eyed him suspiciously.

'And just who would you be?'

Thorne, who had already been fumbling for it, now held out his warrant card. The constable looked at it and nodded.

'I see, sir. Yes, I was keeping watch.'

'Then what the hell are you doing here?' asked Thorne.

The constable said firmly, 'As it happens, I was waved in by my inspector, sir.'

Thorne shook his head in disgust, and muttered rhetorically: 'Why is it always bloody signals that go wrong?'

Then, to Ballantyne: 'That's probably blown it.'

The constable took it upon himself to comment. 'I don't see why, sir. He's there alright. Been there ever since he drove up in his old banger – Rover, I think.'

This was a new one on Thorne. No-one had mentioned to him that Tyndall was motorized. It changed things. Whereas Tyndall could be observed and contained all night if necessary, so long as he had no transport, with a car he could make a break. Thorne made up his mind.

'Right,' he said to Ballantyne, 'get back to the other car. Get the driver to block the T-junction with it.' Then he spoke to the constable. 'And you get back to your post. If you see him move, raise your hand straight up, got that?'

'Yes, sir,' said the constable, who then squeezed back past the car to the lane and started trudging back up a narrow path towards the small hill he had occupied before.

Ballantyne, for his part, got out of the car and began trotting back along the lane. Thorne transferred to the driving seat, started the engine and began once more to crawl forwards.

A few minutes later Thorne passed a field entrance and, as he did so, caught a glimpse of the caravan that he had seen so often before in the frontispiece of Margaret Tyndall's book. It was standing about fifty feet from the gate. Even in the brief instant it took him to pass the gate, Thorne saw that the caravan, not unexpectedly, was in a far more dilapidated state than it had been in the photograph. He also saw an old Rover car parked beside it. He continued past the field entrance a few yards and then stopped his car, switched off the engine and, pocketing the key, climbed out. He had now blocked off the section of lane which represented Rupert's only means of motorized escape from the field.

Thorne left his car and headed for the field entrance. He entered the field cautiously, keeping a sharp eye out, but he saw neither Rupert nor the police who should by now be stationed around the caravan. He estimated that Ballantyne would have reached the other car and that Rupert would therefore be trapped. In any case, Thorne did not intend to let him get anywhere near his car. He proposed to arrest him in the caravan.

Keeping out of sight as much as he could, Thorne approached the caravan. He skirted the old Rover and, when he had positioned himself carefully outside the door to the caravan, raised his hand to knock. With a roar, the Rover's engine sprang to life. Startled, Thorne turned towards it and was in time to see Rupert uncoil from his crouching position on the floor and grasp the wheel. The next moment Rupert had slipped the car into gear and, in a burst of noisy acceleration, had shot away to the field entrance.

Thorne realized what must have happened. Rupert must have seen one of the policemen and then, preparing to make his escape in his car, have heard Thorne's car edging towards him down the lane. He must have devised the clever plan of waiting concealed in his car until the police had reached the caravan and then, as he was now trying to do, giving them the slip and making his escape. But if Ballantyne had reached the lane entrance, Rupert would soon discover that he was trapped.

Thorne watched as Rupert first attempted to turn left out of the field and then, seeing Thorne's car there, swung lurching right as fast as he could. This was not more than fifteen to twenty miles an hour in the narrow lane. Thorne hurried after him, entered his own car, backed it into the field and then set off in pursuit. The big question now was: had Ballantyne reached the T-junction and blocked it in time? And that question was answered in a very few minutes. Rounding a gentle bend, Thorne found himself immediately behind Rupert's old Rover 90 which was now travelling at little better than walking pace. And Thorne saw why. Trotting ahead of it, repeatedly looking back over his shoulder at the menacing shape of the big car he could not escape, was Ballantyne. There were, Thorne estimated, still several hundred yards to go to the T-junction. It occurred to Thorne that he must be taking part in the slowest car chase that had ever been crawled. Thorne braked to a halt so as to avoid increasing the pressure on Rupert. Thorne caught glimpses of Ballantyne and could tell from his increasingly erratic pace, that he was tiring rapidly. Rupert roared behind him in low gear, occasionally lunging forwards a little as if testing whether there was enough space to pass the running policeman. Thorne was wondering how long his patience would last, when something happened which made him despair about the intelligence of some of his fellow officers. The police car at the T-junction ahead, which had become visible round a bend, began to move. Thorne realized what was happening. The driver, seeing the strange procession bearing down on him, had come to the conclusion that it was his duty to block the lane. This was, of course, what Thorne had originally intended. But now what the constable should have done, as Thorne saw it, was to give Rupert as much clearance as possible so that Ballantyne would not be unnecessarily endangered. It was obvious that once Rupert had cleared the lane entrance and was into the B-road beyond, he could soon be overtaken in his ancient vehicle by Thorne or by the other police car.

And now the inevitable happened. Seeing his escape route being blocked ahead, Rupert revved his engine menacingly. Ballantyne, guessing what was about to happen, abandoned his flight and pressed himself as hard as he could against the side of the lane. Rupert accelerated and roared past. The dust rose and for a moment Thorne lost sight of what was going on. Then, as Rupert's car disappeared up the lane, just clearing the narrowing gap at the T-junction, and roaring away down the B-road, Thorne saw Ballantyne lying still on the lane's surface.

Thorne knew what action duty required of him. It demanded that he accelerate, chase Rupert and catch him. His car was not as wide as the old Rover. He could, with care, have passed Ballantyne safely and he knew that as soon as he'd passed him the constable at the T-junction would return to look after Ballantyne. But Thorne did not set off in pursuit. He stopped his car and went to Ballantyne, noticing that the police car ahead was now roaring off in pursuit of the Rover. He found his sergeant unconscious with blood pouring from a gash just below his left knee. The wound have been caused by some sharp projection – possibly the jagged edge of a rusted panel – on the old Rover.

Thorne picked up Ballantyne and carried him to his own car. He laid him on the back seat and then set off to find the nearest hospital.

An hour later, Thorne walked out of a neat little Oxfordshire cottage hospital, comforted by knowing that Ballantyne was not in danger of his life. He had lost a good deal of blood but had been fortunate in not breaking any bones. The doctors were pretty sure that he had no internal injuries either.

18

The party was a great success. In the first place the weather was kind. Milly had made arrangements for holding the whole thing indoors if necessary but that would have strained the resources even of the Queen Anne mansion. In the event contingency plans proved unnecessary. It was a superb summer night.

On a rostrum above the great lawn the cast of 'Owls and Pussycats', the hit London show, enchanted guests by performing some of the show's best numbers. On another part of the lawn a large dance floor had been laid. Around it three top-grade groups played. Two of these were deafening and the third, specially provided for the old folk in their thirties, was merely intolerably loud. The groups played for three hundred guests and another hundred crashers. Milly proudly informed Thorne of the latter figure, apparently believing that the number of crashers was the real gauge of the success of any party.

There were mountains of delicious food and lakes of champagne and other drinks. There was a crescent moon. There was also a fun feature which Milly herself had dreamed up and organized. Every so often throughout the evening a surprise event took place. At one point laser-lit ballet girls, dressed as fairies, descended from a clump of treetops. At another a troupe of clowns came tumbling out of the rhododendrons. But the one event that Thorne was hoping for never occurred. His pocket bleeper did not bleep. He could not understand why not. All that day he had waited for the news that Rupert Tyndall had been captured. But Tyndall had somehow avoided the pursuing car and then had sensibly abandoned his old Rover about ten miles from the T-junction. He had then simply vanished. The area had been combed and recombed for clues and for Rupert but no sign of him, or indication of his direction of travel, had been found. Rupert was not a professional criminal. He would not have had a transfer vehicle waiting. There would have been no safe houses for him to go to. Deprived of the caravan, he was simply a very conspicuous young man on the run. He should have been easy to find.

Ballantyne was recovering in hospital. It was a pity, thought Thorne, that he couldn't be at the party. The young sergeant would have enjoyed it far more than his boss was doing. But Ballantyne had lost a lot of blood and had received a number of transfusions. His condition was not serious and the consultant maintained that he would be fit for discharge in a week or so.

'Great, isn't it?' asked Milly, coming upon Thorne in a quiet spot in the grounds.

She had several times before encountered him in quiet spots in the grounds and wondered why. It had never occurred to her that he was deliberately seeking them out for fear that the din of the speakers would drown out the plaintive electronic summons of his pocket bleeper.

Thorne nodded.

'Have you had a chat with the commissioner?' asked Milly.

Thorne smiled. It had amazed him when the country's second policeman, Sir James Stonemore, had accepted Milly's invitation and it had amazed him even more when he had actually turned up with his wife.

Thorne had, in fact, exchanged a few words with the great man earlier in the evening. The commissioner had disconcerted him by asking unceremoniously:

'Why do you want to be a cop, Thorne, when you're obviously as rich as Croesus?'

Thorne had stammered something horribly sanctimonious about doing his bit for society and had been relieved that Stonemore had merely chuckled knowingly in reply. Nevertheless Thorne had received the impression that both Milly and the party had made a good impression on Sir James.

'Come on, Lance.' said Milly, taking his hand. 'Let's have a dance before the groups pack up.'

Feeling a trifle self-conscious, Thorne allowed her to tug him on to the large parquet floor where fifty or sixty couples were already jerking like the victims of some appalling nervous affliction. Soon Thorne was also twitching in a manner which may have looked quite impressive but which struck him as absurd. He took small pleasure in dancing but a good deal in being able to master any social accomplishment that might prove useful to his career.

By half-past two, Thorne had pretty much abandoned all hope that Rupert would be nabbed that night. Only a handful of couples remained. The car-park had been cleared and the hired servants had started tidying up. Thorne sought out Milly and asked her if she'd mind if he went up to bed. He needed a night's sleep because it seemed that he would have to mobilize a nation-wide manhunt the next day for Rupert Tyndall.

Milly kissed him on the nose and swayed a little. She had consumed a lot of champagne. She told him to go ahead. She would supervise the departure of the final guests and then join him. As he headed for the stairs, Thorne suddenly realized that he was hungry.

Of all the people who had been in the splendid house that evening he was probably the only one who had not eaten a bite. He entered the large drawing room where there were now only two hired girls tidying up. He made himself up a plate of assorted good things and poured a glass of champagne and took them with him upstairs to the master bedroom. There he sat down at the small table and ate his cold supper. Then he went into the bathroom, removing his jacket as he went, and cleaned his teeth. He went back into the bedroom, turned down the bed, got out his pyjamas from under the pillow – and heard a scream. He froze. He thought, but was not certain, that it had been Milly who had screamed. Then he heard it again and this time he knew it was Milly's voice. He moved at great speed, first to the room door and then to the stairhead. Taking the stairs two at a time, he soon reached the marbled hall, darted through it and out on to the porch. And there he saw them: Milly cringing away from a tall young man who was simply standing and looking at her.

So that was why the police had been unable to find Rupert Tyndall. He had been lurking in the grounds of Thorne's house all evening, and perhaps most of the day as well, waiting for the party to end.

Rupert looked at Thorne and said in a pained voice: 'She started screaming for no reason.'

'It's him,' gasped Milly. 'Lance, it's him!'

Thorne realized that Milly had experienced a severe trauma at being suddenly confronted by Rupert, whom she had last seen at the beach house in Norfolk and whom she looked on as a murderer. He knew she might lapse into the shell-shocked condition she had been prone to ever since her Corsican ordeal. Then Thorne became aware that mercifully one of the servants had joined him on the porch, doubtless also attracted by Milly's screams. He turned to her and found it was the catering manager to whom he had been inadvertently rude the previous day when she had arrived with her caravan. Now he asked urgently.

'Could you take Mrs Thorne up to the bedroom?'

'Of course,' said the girl sensibly.

She went over to Milly and took her by the arm. Milly did not resist. She was led into the house. And now Thorne turned to the wanted man and uttered the ritual words: 'Rupert Tyndall, I am taking you into custody – '

'Hang on!' the other urged.

Angrily Thorne tried again: 'I must warn you – '

But again Rupert interrupted: 'Just hang on. Is he alright? That's what I came to find out. The chap I hit. He's not dead, is he?'

Thorne gazed at him severely for a moment but he decided to answer the question: 'No, he's not dead. You're lucky there. He's recovering in hospital.'

Rupert nodded and said:

'That's a relief.'

Thorne had an idea he meant it.

'Alright,' said Rupert. 'Now you can arrest me if you want, superintendent, but I'll tell you one thing: you're going to look bloody silly if you do.'

'Why is that?' asked Thorne, goaded into abandoning the official formula by the confidence in the other's voice.

'Because,' said Rupert fiercely. 'I didn't do it. I didn't even dislike Charles Makepeace.'

'Really?' said Thorne narrowly. 'Then could you explain why your mother thinks that you killed him?'

164

Rupert gave a small, bitter laugh.

'Yes, I could. It's because I told her that I killed him.'

'And why did you tell her that?'

'Because mother's crazy. Haven't you noticed? It's because of Margaret dying young – and dad hanging himself. Even without her stroke, mother's had enough misery to make her a bit crazy. So – she found a scapegoat – Makepeace. She blamed all the family troubles on him. God, you wouldn't believe the pressure I've been under, superintendent. She kept on and on at me, saying that if I was a man I'd avenge my father's death. In the end, chiefly to shut her up, I told her that I had done.'

The voice of intuition, which Thorne trusted, said:

'Truth. He's telling the truth.'

But what he said out loud was.

'Bit risky, wasn't it?'

Rupert shook his head.

'No, not at the time. You see, I didn't know she'd been making those loony phone calls. I thought I was just humouring her and trying to get a little peace for myself. I thought that in a few years, when she was back to normal, I'd tell her the truth.'

'If you're innocent,' said Thorne, 'why did you run?'

'Because you started chasing me. When I found out about mother's hate calls, I suddenly realized that I really might find myself in trouble. Innocent people do end up behind bars. So I took off for the caravan to think things over. But I'm not a killer, superintendent. Why, I don't even kill spiders. I put them out of the house.'

'Come on,' said Thorne. 'Inside. I'm going to phone for assistance. You're nicked, Rupert.'

Rupert looked disbelieving.

'So you still – '

But Thorne cut in quickly.

'For causing grievous bodily harm to my sergeant.'

'Oh, I see,' said Rupert. Then, after a pause, he said, 'And what about Makepeace?'

'Strangely enough,' said Thorne. 'I might just be able to help you with that one. But it'll have to keep until the morning. Let's go.'

Thorne had Rupert Tyndall put on ice overnight in the lock-up of the local police station. The next morning he drove him, handcuffed to a constable, to London and took him straight to the Makepeace cottage. He indicated the passage beside the garage along which the intruder, according to the sole witness, had entered the house.

'Could you get along there?' he asked, removing the handcuffs.

'I doubt it,' said Tyndall.

But when he tried, he found that he could. However, because of his size and broad shoulders, he could only do it by edging sideways. The old lady had not reported any such technique.

'How about that wall?' said Thorne, pointing to the wall beside it. 'Could you get on to it?'

Rupert smiled.

'No problem,' he said.

He put up his hands and in a trice was on the wall. Thorne was satisfied. If Rupert Tyndall had been the intruder, he would not have edged laboriously along the alley. He'd have been up on the wall and into the house in a matter of moments. The practical test only confirmed what he'd already decided: that Rupert Tyndall was not the murderer of Charles Makepeace.

19

Two days later, Thorne visited Ballantyne in the small Oxfordshire hospital. The sergeant was wearing a dressing gown over pyjamas. Both garments had been supplied by the hospital and did not fit too well.

The two policemen walked together in the corridors outside Ballantyne's ward.

'What will Tyndall get, sir?' asked Ballantyne.

'For cutting you up? Well, a good brief will probably get him off with a suspended sentence. He'll argue that Tyndall naturally panicked when we chased him, and that we had no business chasing him in the first place. And we didn't, did we?'

'You feel quite sure he didn't kill Makepeace?'

'Everything he said rang true. I think he's in the clear. Now when can we expect to see you back on the job?'

The sergeant grinned.

'I'm in no particular hurry, sir. After all I get three square meals a day and – '

But he had misjudged his superior's mood.

'I need you, sergeant,' interrupted Thorne harshly.

'I believe they're discharging me tomorrow morning, sir,' said Ballantyne quickly.

Thorne nodded.

'Good, then you can start leaning on Ali.'

'Ali?' repeated Ballantyne, in a surprised tone of voice.

'That's right. To help us nail Musquat Singh.'

'You think Singh did it, sir?' asked Ballantyne cautiously.

Thorne sighed.

'I think he's the best suspect we've got left. I need this one, sergeant. If we don't catch the bastard, I may as well leave the force and take up polo.'

'Ali's being watched, isn't he, sir? Anything useful there?'

Thorne shook his head dejectedly.

'He visits his father who runs a curry parlour in the East End and his girl-friend. There's just one funny thing – '

'Yes?' prompted Ballantyne.

'It's the relationship between Singh and Ali's father. Now Singh as we know is quite seriously rich and Ali's father is poor. But in some ways they're like brothers. Singh pays Ali's father a regular pension and he's training up Ali to be a wizard like himself. Still none of that suggests that Singh poisoned Makepeace, does it?'

'I wouldn't have thought so, sir,' said Ballantyne diplomatically.

'Right, pressure Ali a bit when you get out of here. Try and get a lead on whoever was with Singh on the night of the break-in.'

'Yes, sir,' said Ballantyne.

But in the event he never did. It proved unnecessary. For the very next morning, the plain-clothes man who was keeping tabs on Ali's movements apparently made a breakthrough.

The constable was seated in a venerable orange mini about fifty yards up the street from the driveway to Musquat Singh's house when he saw a mini-cab pull into the driveway. A few minutes later, it emerged again, this time with Ali in the back. The constable

168

was new on the detail. He didn't know that this was unusual and that Ali had never before been seen to take a mini cab. So it was without any special feeling that the constable let the cab get some way ahead and then pulled out and followed it. Before long, it became fairly clear where it was going. The constable had been briefed and he realized that they were heading for 'The Star of India', the restaurant owned and run by Ali's father, off Brick Lane in the East End of London. In due course, the mini cab pulled up there with the tailing constable close behind. The policeman drove past and turned into a convenient side street, where he left his mini. He walked back on the opposite side of the street from the restaurant and found a place from where he could watch events without being too conspicuous.

At this time of the morning 'The Star of India' was still closed. Indeed a 'closed' sign hung on the door. Through a large plate glass window, and despite the fact that there were no lights on in the restaurant, the policeman could dimly see Ali arguing with an older Indian who, he realized, was probably the boy's father. Ali was brandishing a large envelope at the older man who was apparently rejecting it with dismay. The envelope was long and fat and suggested the possibility that it might be stuffed with banknotes. The constable watched the row for some time. In the end Ali won. The older Indian took the envelope with obvious distaste, glanced about and luckily failed to spot the observing policeman. He then carried the envelope with him behind the counter and simply disappeared. At least that was what it looked like. The watching policeman soon realized that the old man must have crouched down. When he rose again he was no longer holding the envelope. Clearly it had been hidden somewhere behind the counter.

Realizing the potential importance of what he'd seen the constable made his way as quickly as possible to his mini and manned the radio. He asked for Thorne or Ballantyne but, as luck would have it, neither was available. Thorne had gone to Paddington to meet Ballantyne's train. The sergeant was returning to duty after his stay in the Oxfordshire hospital, and when the surveillance man phoned, he and Thorne both were out of radio contact. Learning this, the constable told the duty officer what he'd observed at 'The Star of India', and asked for instructions. The duty officer drew a blank at finding anyone else from Thorne's team on the premises and instructed the constable to obey his standing orders. This meant that the constable, against his better judgement, followed Ali when he left 'The Star of India' rather than staying with Ali's father and the mysterious envelope.

When Thorne and Ballantyne, having stopped in the station for breakfast, finally heard of the message an hour later, Thorne instantly recognized its importance. He gave instructions for a search warrant to be obtained and for a stake-out on 'The Star of India' to be mounted. But it was not until nearly lunchtime that he and Ballantyne were on their way to the restaurant.

'Two hours,' said Thorne bitterly. 'Two hours to get a search warrant.'

'Still, we know the packet's still in the restaurant, sir,' said Ballantyne soothingly.

'Not for certain, we don't,' Thorne contradicted him. 'There was a gap of an hour before I could set up surveillance. The bloody assassin could have come for his money and left with it.'

170

'Why didn't Jenkins stay there?' asked Ballantyne, referring to the plain-clothes man in the mini.

'His orders were to stay with Ali. He left when Ali did.'

'Anyway,' said Ballantyne. 'We can't be sure the money was intended for a hit man. Come to that we can't be sure the envelope had money in it.'

'Oh, it was money,' said Thorne. 'I'll stake my pension on it.'

A quarter of an hour later, Thorne and Ballantyne waited impatiently as a very thin and rather stooped Indian gentleman, who appeared to be in his early fifties, shuffled across the restaurant to admit them. Ali's father peered through the glass and Thorne was sure he detected a faint look of alarm on his face. It was only after Thorne had pointed meaningfully to the lock that the owner of 'The Star of India' with apparent reluctance at last opened the door and let them in.

'Mr Patel?' asked Thorne sharply. 'Mr Harji Patel?'

The Indian nodded.

'Yes?' he asked cautiously.

Thorne and Ballantyne both displayed their warrant cards and Thorne said: 'We're police officers.'

Mr Patel said, 'Police officers? But I have not requested police assistance.'

His English was fluent but heavily accented. His voice was sprightly, indeed humorous. Thorne felt a slight pulse of sympathy for the frail old Indian, but he pushed past him roughly, saying: 'We have a warrant to search your premises.'

Mr Patel closed the door carefully and then followed them.

'Search?' he echoed. 'Search? Well, I can tell you where the rice and curry powder are kept. There's nothing else here.'

'Don't get clever with me, Mr Patel,' said Thorne. 'This morning, at approximately 10.15 A.M., your son, Ali, was seen to hand you an envelope containing money.'

Ballantyne reacted with a slight look of dismay to this assertion. There was no way Thorne could be sure that the envelope had contained money. Harji Patel apparently felt this too. He grinned.

'Money?' he exclaimed incredulously. 'Ali has no money. I only wish he had.'

'Where is the envelope?' asked Thorne.

Patel shrugged.

'I cannot tell you about what does not exist. Oh, it is true that Ali did call here. He brought some jasmine tea, which I am very fond of. It was a present from his master, Mr Musquat Singh, my old friend who is so very kind to me and who – '

Thorne interrupted brusquely, turning to Ballantyne and saying sharply:

'The envelope was hidden behind the counter, probably at floor level. Find it, please, sergeant.'

At this Harji Patel looked distinctly anxious. He said quickly: 'Just what are you looking for, inspector?'

'Superintendent,' corrected Thorne.

'I beg your pardon, superintendent,' amended Patel. 'But if I knew what this was all about, perhaps I could save you some time.'

Thorne said brutally, 'We're looking for money intended for paying a hired assassin. That is what the money was for, isn't it?'

'No, certainly not!' said Patel.

Thorne guessed that Ballantyne would not be too happy about the way he was handling Patel, but it was getting results.

'Then you admit there is money.' Thorne pounced triumphantly.

Patel, realizing his error, flapped his arms feebly.

'Well – money. There is money in the till – a little. That is the only money in the place.'

At that moment, Ballantyne, reaching beneath the sink, found a panel that was obviously loose. Not much manipulation was needed to release it. Behind it Ballantyne found a shoebox-sized space which seemed to be packed with papers. He pulled out a handful of them and the very top one turned out to be a bulging envelope.

'Sir!' said Ballantyne urgently.

Thorne turned. Ballantyne straightened up and handed his chief the envelope. Thorne did not bother to look inside it but simply held it up for Patel's inspection.

'What's in this, Mr Patel?' he asked sternly.

'I have no idea,' said Patel jerkily. And now he actually sounded frightened. 'Where did that come from? I have never seen it. I do not know. What can I – Alright, I tell you the truth, superintendent. It is money. But it is – it is a present to buy a new – a new television.'

Thorne smiled briefly. He tore open the envelope and flipped through the stack of notes inside.

'An expensive television, Mr Patel,' he remarked ironically. 'There must be several thousand pounds here.'

'Yes, but – but – you see – '

'I see that you could be an accessory to murder,' said Thorne solemnly.

Patel actually drew back a pace. He paled beneath the chestnut of his complexion.

'No, no, you do not understand. Murder? No, it is –
it is, I – '

But to Thorne's annoyance Ballantyne picked this
moment to interrupt.

'Sir,' exclaimed the sergeant. 'Sir, I think you should
look at these.'

Ballantyne had been quickly examining some of the
other documents he had found under the sink.

'Not now, sergeant.' Thorne returned to the attack:
'Now, Mr Patel – '

But once more Ballantyne interrupted: 'But, sir,
they have a bearing on the case. An important one.'

He held out what were clearly cuttings from old
newspapers. Thorne glanced at them. It was obvious,
from the brittle and yellowing state of the paper itself,
that any news the cuttings contained was now ancient
history.

'They're more than thirty years old,' Ballantyne
specified. 'The stories are about illegal immigrants. It
seems a boatload went down in the channel. It was
thought there were some survivors but they were never
captured.'

As he listened to Ballantyne's words, the Indian
restaurant keeper, Harji Patel, hung his head in a
despondent gesture. Thorne took the cuttings from
Ballantyne and glanced through them. He sighed.

'So that's what this is all about,' he said sadly.
'Blackmail.'

A little more questioning sufficed to fill in the
picture. Musquat Singh and Harji Patel it seemed,
were illegal immigrants, blackbirds, as they had been
known in the Fifties. That was obviously the source of
the bond between them. Patel had brought up his son
Ali without ever telling him of his own illegal status.
Patel himself had never met the blackmailer. It had,

of course, been the blackmailer, come to collect his annual pay-off, whom Ali had heard in Musquat Singh's office on the night of the break-in. By mentioning it, Ali had thought he was providing his master with an alibi but Musquat Singh had realized that he would be more likely to steer the police towards discovery of his illegal status.

Ultimately, after Ballantyne began to press Ali, Singh had told the truth to the young man. It was then that Ali had retracted his earlier allegation. There were, however, important details that Harji could not tell them. One of these was the identity of the blackmailer.

Thorne officially notified Patel that the information would be passed to the Home Office for action. Then he and Ballantyne went in search of Musquat Singh, millionaire and blackbird, to get the final details.

A little later, in Singh's ornate home in Highgate, Thorne asked the astrologer:

'And who was he? This blackmailer?'

Singh smiled.

'A Scottish fisherman. He brought us over in his boat. For a long time I thought Harji and I were the only survivors. It was a most terrible storm. Then after some years the fisherman turned up and said he had become frightened of the sea and he expected me to support him. I have done just that for more than ten years.'

'And how did he find you?'

'From a photo in a Sunday paper. When I began to be known as an astrologer.'

Thorne nodded.

'I take it you've always looked after Harji because he saved your life in the storm?'

Musquat Singh smiled.

'Oh no, Harji had a much stronger claim on me than that.'

Thorne was surprised.

'Really? What?'

'I saved his,' said Singh. 'A great mistake. They become like your children. And now, ironically, I will be deported but Harji will be allowed to stay because he has an English son.'

'I'm sorry,' said Thorne. 'But if it's any comfort to you we'll put your fisherman behind bars first.'

'If you catch him.'

'We're bound to. Now that you've given us his address. Probably within hours rather than days.'

'It is some comfort,' admitted Singh. 'As for being deported – I don't mind too much. I'm getting a bit homesick for my native land. I think I would like to go to India and set up an institute for paranormal research. Am I under arrest, superintendent?'

'No, I don't think that will be necessary,' said Thorne. 'But naturally I shall have to lay my information before the Home Office.'

'Naturally,' agreed Musquat Singh.

Thorne and Ballantyne turned to leave. Then Thorne turned back. It was an improper question for a police officer to ask but Thorne couldn't resist.

'Incidentally,' he began.

'Yes?' said Musquat Singh.

'Didn't your own horoscope warn you that this would happen?'

Musquat Singh smiled. 'We never cast our own horoscopes,' he explained. 'It's considered unlucky.'

20

'Why did you turn left, Lance?' asked Milly frowning.

'I just wanted to check something out,' returned Thorne laconically.

They were on their way to a dinner party at a fine house near the Whitestone Pond, which crowns the Northern heights of London.

'Check what out?' asked Milly. Then both reproach and incredulity filled her voice. 'Hell, I don't believe this. You mean something connected with the case? Right?'

'It'll only take a couple of minutes,' said Thorne soothingly.

'For God's sake, Lance, can't you take one evening off? We're going to a dinner party!'

'We've got a little time in hand,' insisted Thorne. 'Anyway here we are.'

He pulled into the small square where the Makepeace cottage was situated and parked on the opposite side of the road from it. Milly had never been there before. She looked about her without enthusiasm.

'So? Where the hell are we?' she asked peevishly.

'This is where the break-in happened,' explained Thorne.

'Really?' returned Milly sarcastically. 'That's just great! I've always wanted to see where the break-in happened!'

'Calm down, Milly,' urged Thorne, with a touch of annoyance. 'Look, I'm a detective. I've got a case that's getting away from me – '

He stopped abruptly. A plum-red Rolls-Royce had slipped quietly into the square and was pulling up at the cottage across the road.

'What the hell – ' exclaimed Thorne. He stared hard. The man at the wheel was clearly not a chauffeur. He was alone in the car. A moment later he opened his door and began to descend from the splendid vehicle. Thorne exclaimed incredulously: 'Sir Max Sillmann!'

Because of parked vehicles in the square, Thorne had so far felt secure from being seen. But Sir Max, having got out of the Rolls, paused and gazed around keenly. Thorne instantly turned and swept Milly into his arms so that Sir Max, if he saw them, would take them for lovers. After a moment or two, he whispered in her ear.

'Has he gone?'

'He's gone,' returned Milly sourly, 'and so has part of my upper lip.'

'I'm sorry, darling,' Thorne returned, 'but I didn't want him to see me.'

'Don't tell me. It was the murderer, right?' asked Milly.

'Who knows?' said Thorne wearily. 'What I do know is that it was the boss of Carr Sillmann. What I want to know is: why is he calling on the victim's wife?'

'How banal,' said Milly. 'You're suggesting he killed the husband to get at the wife?'

'Wouldn't be the first time,' returned Thorne.

'But, Lance, they're both over sixty!' exclaimed Milly incredulously.

'I know. But their instincts could be in working order.'

'You're not serious.'

'It's a lead,' said Thorne. 'And there are not too many of those about.'

Milly sighed resignedly.

'What now?' she asked. 'Are we on a stake-out?'

Thorne looked at her thoughtfully.

'You realize,' he said warningly, 'it could take hours.'

She gazed at him in amazement.

'I was kidding, for God's sake!'

'Right, right,' muttered Thorne as he started the engine.

The next morning Thorne said to Ballantyne, 'I want you to check up on Sir Max Sillman and Isobel Makepeace. Try and find out if there is, or ever has been, an attachment between them.'

'What kind of attachment?' asked Ballantyne.

'A romantic one, naturally,' specified Thorne.

'But – ' said Ballantyne with a puzzled look. 'I mean – are you thinking of a *crime passionnel*, sir?'

'Oh, very classy,' said Thorne sarcastically. 'I wish I knew Greek too. But – yes, that is what I'm thinking of, sergeant.'

'They're not young, sir,' said Ballantyne dubiously.

'What's the matter with everyone?' exclaimed Thorne, thinking of Milly's scepticism of the night before. 'People don't stop fancying other people just because they're getting on a bit. Look, last night I observed Sir Max Sillmann, looking very like a suitor, entering the Makepeace cottage. Conceivably he was just there to deliver the dividends but I still want it checked out. *Entendu, mon vieux*?'

'Of course, sir,' said Ballantyne promptly.

Ballantyne checked it out and discovered something surprising. It seemed that Sir Max and Isobel Makepeace had lived together for a year when they were both very young and before they had met their future spouses. On the strength of this discovery, Thorne went with Ballantyne for a talk with Sir Max Sillmann.

Once Sir Max had seated them, none too cordially, Thorne began: 'Would you mind telling me, sir, about your relationship with Mrs Isobel Makepeace?'

'Isobel?' said Sir Max gruffly. 'I have no relationship with Isobel. Superintendent, if you have nothing material to ask me, could I induce you to be quick? I have several important decisions to make before I shut up shop this evening.'

'You used Mrs Makepeace's first name?'

'Yes, of course I did. I have known her for a long time. She is not only the wife of one of my oldest colleagues but a friend as well.'

'And that is all?'

'Yes, of course. What else are you implying?'

'Does the street address "47, Dahomey Close" mean anything to you?'

That it meant something to Sir Max Sillmann was perfectly obvious. He literally gave a gasp of astonishment and then seemed to collapse slightly, like a burst balloon. He nodded slowly:

'I see,' he said gravely. 'How did you find out?'

'It wasn't difficult, once we'd decided to look. I believe that it's the address of the terraced house in Kentish Town that you shared with Isobel Duncan, as she then was, for nearly two years when you were both in your twenties?'

Sir Max smiled faintly.

'It doesn't exist any more. I was near it the other day and went to have a look. Dahomey Close doesn't exist either. It's got buried and the gravestone is one of those vast brick housing estates with elevated walks and suchlike. When Isobel and I lived there, it was nice. Just a working-class terrace but with cheerful little gardens. It was all we could afford. I was learning to be a banker and she was learning art. I became a banker but she never became an artist.'

'May I ask why you have concealed this relationship?'

'I didn't conceal – '

'Before you go on, sir. I have several times asked you the exact nature of your relationship with Mrs Isobel Makepeace and you have never mentioned this obviously very significant aspect of it.'

Sir Max nodded ruefully.

'What is the point of raking up the past? No-one else knows about it. It would upset my wife. Besides – do you know what banking is all about, superintendent?'

'Money, sir?'

Sir Max shook his head sadly.

'No. No more than flying is about air. Banking is about confidence. It is not true that the Rothschilds, who were the first and greatest merchant bankers, really were divine as some people have suggested. They just modelled themselves on God. You see, people will let any scoundrel look after their homes, their children, even their own bodies. But their money? Only God is good enough. And a womanizer, even one who has reformed after youthful indiscretions, is a long way from God. Does that answer your question, superintendent?'

'I'm not sure, sir. You're saying that the relationship with Mrs Makepeace was over a long time ago?'

'Exactly.'

'Why did it end?'

It did not need a detective to note the shifty look that immediately appeared on Sir Max's face. But then it cleared as the veteran banker faced his past.

'Alright. It ended because we were poor. I needed a leg-up if I was going to become a force in the City. I met a woman – a rich woman – '

'So you threw Isobel Makepeace over in order to marry money?' asked Thorne with calculated brutality.

But Sir Max shook his head sadly.

'She insisted. She knew we would be miserable if I were thwarted all my life. Perhaps I should say this very clearly – we were not in love. We had never talked of marriage. I met her in a queue for the cinema and we were young and both in need of a place to live. It was a sensible arrangement as much as a love affair.'

'Did you marry her off to Charles Makepeace?'

'You could say that. Much later, of course. She remained single for years. When I began to succeed I helped her to start her business. I gave her advice and later I introduced her to Charles, having told her he might be right. And he was. They've been together for a long time.

'Happily?'

Sir Max shrugged wearily.

'How many marriages are happy?'

'Is yours?'

'Not specially. But it is seasoned. It will take the strain. We have two sons. Grown-up but sons.'

'And there is nothing more between you and Isobel Makepeace?'

Sir Max shook his head positively.

'In that case, sir, could you explain why you were observed entering her cottage last Tuesday evening at about half-past eight?'

Sir Max nodded bitterly.

'So you've had me followed? Did you peek through the curtains too? If you had you'd have seen me signing papers. I have been helping Isobel to get back into business. Against my better judgement if you want to know. Charles left her a comfortable income but she is bored. You must be aware, if you have been following me, that we have dined out together three times, two lunches and a dinner. And if you have been following me closely, you will also have seen that Isobel apparently retains some vestiges of romantic feeling for me. But that – '

And it was then that Sir Max abruptly stopped and gazed from Thorne to Ballantyne and back incredulously.

'But wait – wait. I begin to see. You think our behaviour is guilty, is that it? You think that we – in some ghastly conspiracy – poisoned Charles so that we could get back together? Is that it, superintendent?'

Thorne looked straight into his eyes.

'Did you and Isobel Makepeace murder her husband, sir?'

Sir Max sighed deeply.

'No, superintendent. I don't suppose there was ever the capability for murder in either of us. But if there ever was it has burned out a long time ago. We are too near our own ends to plan anyone else's. I see now the wisdom of not lying to the police. I did it out of simple discretion – second nature to a banker. As a result you have added us to your list of suspects. Well, I can only protest our innocence, superintendent. I don't suppose I could prove it.'

'Thank you, sir,' said Thorne, manifestly concluding the interview.

'What do you think?' asked Ballantyne when they were back in their car.

'I think murders have been committed for lesser motives. But there is a big objection.'

'What he said, sir? They're too old to be killers?'

183

'Not sure about that. There are homicidal geriatrics in the world. But the murder scenario has one big flaw. Let's follow it through. Sir Max and Isobel Makepeace were deeply in love. However, for practical reasons, they each married someone else. They found that they still loved each other and went on yearning to be together. So far so good. But then, after having lived forty years apart, is it conceivable that they would plot to kill one of the two spouses who stood between them, and risk all they possessed and their liberty as well, when that person was, as we both knew, in such rotten physical shape that he was unlikely to live another year?'

'Doesn't seem very likely, does it, sir?' agreed Ballantyne sombrely.

'So who have we got left?' asked Thorne grimly.

'Tucker, sir,' answered Ballantyne.

'Tucker,' repeated Thorne with a sigh. 'We keep going back to Tucker because he knows about poisons. But we also know that if Makepeace had lived a little longer, he would have signed a document giving Tucker more funds. In other words, Tucker logically should have tried to keep his old friend alive, not killed him.'

'You really believe they were old friends, sir?' asked Ballantyne.

'That's what everyone says, including people who have known them for years. Still, I suppose we'd better go and have another chat with him. We're getting near the bottom of the barrel.'

21

Above Tucker's head behind his desk was a rack which had clearly been specially designed and built. It held about a hundred and fifty small phials of liquid, some of them brilliantly coloured. Thorne knew that each of these phials contained a different industrial poison. It was a fascinating display.

'Did you and Charles Makepeace ever quarrel?' asked Thorne bluntly.

'Not that I recall,' returned Colin Tucker thoughtfully. 'We were a damned good team in the navy. In recent years we didn't see that much of each other but we remained friends. And then, of course, Charles helped me to start my company and invested substantially in it.'

'I believe you had a bad patch about six months ago,' said Thorne pointedly.

Tucker nodded and said wryly:

'I was overextended. I'd hired too many new reps, opened small offices and laboratories – even smaller than this one – in Birmingham and Glasgow. Had to remortgage the house.'

'And did you ask Makepeace for help?'

'Oh yes,' said Tucker. 'And he gave it. It took him a little while to raise the money but then he put up quite substantial sums.'

Thorne changed the subject.

'What do you know about phenylzine, Mr Tucker?'

Tucker smiled sadly and said:

'That's why you're here, isn't it, superintendent? I

assume that was the poison that killed Charley. Yes, of course I know about it. It's prescribed for depression under various brand names. But if I wanted to poison someone, superintendent, I wouldn't use phenylzine.'

'Really? What would you use?'

'Oh, I don't know. There are some new organic compounds which are very quickly metabolized by the body. I think it should be possible to put together a cocktail of those that would be virtually indetectable.'

Thorne nodded.

'You're very authoritative, Mr Tucker, I'm surprised we don't use you as a consultant.'

'Oh, but you do, superintendent,' Tucker corrected him gently. 'Well, the Yard does. You're City, aren't you?' Then he sighed deeply. 'Superintendent, Charles Makepeace was not only my friend but my benefactor. I don't want to sound wimpish but I'd have done my best to stop anyone harming him.'

'I understand, Mr Tucker.'

'And as I think you already know,' Tucker continued, 'if Charley had lived only a few weeks longer, I would have benefited greatly from additional investment.'

'I am aware of that,' said Thorne. 'Well then – thank you for your cooperation.'

The two detectives departed.

'Same problem,' said Thorne in the car. 'No motive. Ideal suspect but no motive. In fact a negative motive. Everything he said has been checked out. It's all true. If Tucker was the one who put the poison in the flask he did himself a lot of harm at the same time.'

'So you think he's innocent, sir?'

'I think it looks as if he's innocent,' said Thorne grimly.

'So who's left?' asked Ballantyne anxiously.

'The women,' said Thorne with a sigh. 'But first, let's turn to the computer, the copper's best friend – after his intuition.'

At ten past seven that evening, footsteps still sounded occasionally in the corridor outside Thorne's door. But most of the superintendent's colleagues had left for the night. Thorne sat gazing at a chart on the computer screen ahead of him. It gave a breakdown of all possible sources of the poison phenylzine. None of the suspects they had considered would have had much difficulty, Thorne had concluded, in obtaining the stuff. It would have been easiest for Tucker but his alibi was the strongest. That was the trouble with this case. It was self-cancelling.

Since the favourites had, for the time being anyway, been eliminated, what about an outsider? Thorne sighed. The outsiders included, just for starters, all three hundred of the staff at Carr Sillmann. Repeated computer searches had failed to narrow them down significantly.

Thorne punched a button and the computer image changed. The display now showed both graphic and schematic breakdowns of Stella Tyson's story. A moment after this came up on the screen the phone rang. Thorne answered it with a curt: 'Thorne here?'

'Lance? What the hell are you doing?' came his wife's reproachful voice.

'How do you mean?' asked Thorne mildly, his glance continuing to play over the screen display.

'Why aren't you home? I've made a duck.'

'A duck?' repeated Thorne, while still thinking about Stella Tyson. She and Makepeace, he recalled, had had lunch in Wendover and then had driven to a layby where Makepeace had pointed out a folly to her. They'd drunk a toast from his hip flask –

'A duck! Quack quack!' said Milly crossly, interrupting his train of thought. 'With black cherries. Lance, are you doped up or something?'

'Look, I'm sorry,' said Thorne apologetically. 'But I told you I'd be here all night.'

'No, you didn't,' answered Milly indignantly. 'Tonight we were going to have this duck.'

Thorne wanted to conclude the conversation but on a friendly note. He knew that Milly had been having a hard time with him recently. He had, however, no recollection of having discussed dinner arrangements with her. And he was finding it difficult to focus his thoughts on anything other than the subject that had been obsessing him for the last forty-eight hours. Wendover, the folly, the hip flask –

'Look, Milly,' Thorne tried again. 'I can't leave my office now. I've only got the use of the computer until tomorrow.' This was, of course, a diplomatic lie. 'I'm near the breakthrough.'

'Are you, Lance? Well, I'm near the point where I phone the airport and get me a ticket to Boston.'

'Boston?' asked Lance trying to take in her meaning.

'That's right. And if I do, I shall go there and spend the rest of the summer with my mother.'

He gave what he hoped would emerge as a regretful sigh.

'Well, alright, darling,' he said sadly, 'if that's what you want – '

Her voice came back, sounding deeply hurt. 'You'd let me, wouldn't you?' she asked incredulously.

Thorne tried to rally.

'Milly, I don't want you to – of course, I don't. But if you feel you need a change.'

Now her voice was charged with anger.

'The change I need is to see you sometimes. God-damn it, you're my husband, Lance – '

'True, Milly, but I'm also a – '

He broke off. It had come to him in a flash – a way of harmonizing this situation.

'Well?' asked Milly. 'You're also what? A cop? Hell, I know you're a cop. Even at weekends you never stop being a cop.'

'You're right, Milly,' said Thorne with what he hoped would sound like sincere remorse. 'Alright, tomorrow's Saturday. I'll stop being a cop. We'll have lunch together.'

'Lunch?' asked Milly suspiciously. 'What do you mean?'

'Let's drive out in the country and have lunch in Wendover.'

'Wendover? Why Wendover?'

'First-rate restaurant there. Been meaning to try it. And I feel like getting out of town. It's the Cherry Tree restaurant – opposite the town hall. Meet me there at one, Milly, and we'll have a good lunch.'

'But hang on, Lance. Why can't we have lunch in town – or here at home? Why does it have to be – '

'Good,' said Lance decisively. 'See you at one.'

And he hung up.

He waited tensely for a few minutes, expecting her to call back. But she didn't. He wondered why not and decided she must have believed him when he'd said the Cherry Tree was the in place to dine. The real reason never occurred to him. It was simply that Milly was longing to see him and didn't really mind where.

The Cherry Tree restaurant in Wendover proved to be a tolerable chintzy establishment. Its home-made steak, kidney and mushroom pie was excellent but any

189

dishes more ambitious tended to be disappointing. The service was strong on civility and speed but weak on information. The pretty local girls who scuttled around the tables had a way of blinking at you in hurt surprise if you did anything so unsporting as, for example, inquire what the *soupe de jour* was. Thorne was silent throughout most of the meal. This did not matter since Milly talked non-stop. She told Thorne all about an island in the Aegean owned by a girl-friend. The girl-friend had inherited the island from a former husband as part of a divorce settlement. It was only a small island with three houses on it, but one of those three was a luxurious villa with a swimming pool and all mod cons. Milly had received a letter that very morning from her friend offering her the use of it for a fortnight during the summer. Milly was trying to interest Thorne in the idea. But it was only over coffee that she dared to test her advocacy by asking:

'So what do you think, Lance?'

'About what?' he asked.

'The villa,' answered Milly a trifle irritably. 'Is there any chance you could get away?'

'Certainly there is,' he returned. 'A very good chance. But I've got to put this case to bed first. What did you think of the food, Milly?'

Milly screwed up her face. 'Not so hot, Lance,' she admitted.

'That's what I think too,' said Thorne. 'So would a merchant banker come here?'

Milly stared at him in astonishment.

'Merchant banker? What merchant banker?' she asked.

'If a merchant banker was taking his mistress out to propose to her, is this the sort of place he'd choose?'

Milly gazed at him in dawning dismay.

'Mistress?' she repeated. 'I don't think I believe this.'

Thorne suddenly realized that he might have been a little tactless. He smiled winningly and said: 'It's been fun, Milly. We must do it more often.'

But it was too late. Milly said, in a tight voice: 'This place is connected with the case, isn't it?'

Thorne tried to shrug it off.

'Not directly – ' he began.

But Milly hurried on.

'You weren't taking me out to lunch, were you? You were doing some kind of goddamn reconstruction, right, Mr Future Top Cop?'

She was getting a bit shrill. Thorne glanced around.

'Take it easy, darling,' he urged. 'I'm killing two birds with one stone.'

'Lance, if you go on like this, you're going to kill this particular bird stone dead.'

'Just go along with it this once, Milly,' he pleaded. 'And I'll tell you what: I'll try and find a month for the island later in the year.'

Milly looked at him hard.

'Are you just saying that, Lance?'

'No way,' he said firmly. 'Now, let's go and have a look at this beauty spot.'

'What beauty spot?' she asked, still deeply suspicious.

'Where the dead man proposed to his mistress and they drank a toast out of his hip flask to celebrate.'

'Oh,' said Milly, '*that* beauty spot.'

Lance grinned at her and called for the bill.

Twenty minutes later, Thorne, who had made the trip out to Wendover by train, pulled into a long, landscaped lay-by at the wheel of Milly's Jaguar. The lay-by was situated off a B-road just below the crest of a wooded hill that commanded a breathtaking view of rolling countryside reaching to the horizon. Immediately below them was a belt of forest about a half-mile wide through which, at one point, a church tower protruded. They could see several villages in the middle distance and beyond them a huge cement works which, because of the distance, seemed quite romantic. Cloud shadows surged majestically across the entire landscape.

'Terrific view,' said Milly, when they had descended from the car and were surveying it.

'It is, isn't it?' agreed Thorne. 'But where's the pyramid?'

'Pyramid?' asked Milly in surprise.

'A folly shaped like a pyramid,' explained Thorne. 'The victim pointed it out to his intended. Now do you see any house that looks like a pyramid?'

'Let's go to the other end,' suggested Milly. 'Perhaps you can see it from there.'

They strolled along the lay-by, pausing for a few minutes to sit on one of the raised benches thoughtfully provided by the local council for people enjoying the scenic delights. But there was no sign of Daisy Wilson's pyramid folly.

'Odd,' said Thorne.

They turned at the extremity of the lay-by and set off back towards the Jaguar. Thorne noticed that, while they had been walking away from their car, a red post-office van had drawn up beside it. As they got closer they saw that the driver was eating a sandwich and reading a newspaper.

'I'll just have a word with him,' said Thorne.

Thorne approached the van. So intent was the driver on his racing column, as Thorne perceived when he was very close, that he did not register Thorne until the detective announced himself by clearing his throat. Then the driver looked up sharply.

'Oh yes?' he asked, with a friendly but alert look.

'I wonder,' said Thorne. 'Do you know this area?'

The driver smiled.

'I should do. I've been on the same round for three years now.'

'Well,' said Thorne. 'I heard that there was a house shaped like a pyramid – '

The driver nodded at once.

'Daisy Wilson's house,' he confirmed. 'Famous that is. She was a – you know, someone that writes plays. The house is down there.'

He pointed down towards the sea of treetops beneath them. Thorne frowned.

'Can't actually see it,' he remarked.

'Well, you wouldn't,' confirmed the driver. 'Wrong time of year. Can't see the house because of the trees. To see it, you'll have to go down the lane, past the curve there – '

He pointed.

'It's about a mile and a half,' he amplified.

Thorne looked in the direction the driver was pointing and then back at the man's face.

'Wait a minute,' he said. 'Are you saying that Daisy Wilson's house is not actually visible from here?'

The other shook his head.

'Not when the trees are in leaf. See it plain in winter.'

'See it plain – ' repeated Thorne in a vague sort of way and then he broke off.

'If you want directions – ' the driver resumed.

But Thorne was no longer listening to him. In fact he had turned a trifle rudely, it appeared, and was walking slowly away from the man, deep in thought.

Milly, seeing that Thorne had left the vicinity of the van, approached him.

'Lance, just suppose – ' she began.

He said sharply.

'Quiet!'

And so peremptory was his tone that Milly instantly became silent. She stood still and watched him. He walked hesitantly for a few steps and then half-turned. Milly sensed that he was moving without any purpose or rather that he was moving simply because he needed some bodily accompaniment to his racing thoughts. He came to a halt and stood for a moment as if frozen. And then he began to laugh, softly at first and then more energetically. So bizarre was his appearance that Milly felt a spasm of anxiety.

'Lance? What is it?' she cried. 'What's happened?'

He turned towards her, his eyes actually running with tears. He said: 'I've done it, Milly.'

'Done what?' she asked.

'I've solved it. With your help.' And then he pointed discreetly towards the van driver. 'And with his help. I've got the answer. I know who killed Charles Makepeace and I know why.'

But then the triumphant expression slowly left his face and a frown of concentration replaced it.

'But it could be one hell of a job proving it.'

22

'How did it go at Wendover, sir?' asked Ballantyne the following morning.

Thorne looked at him narrowly.

'The folly was invisible,' he said.

Ballantyne was clearly nonplussed by this pronouncement.

'The folly – ?' he repeated uncertainly.

Thorne broke in impatiently.

'The folly shaped like a pyramid. That Makepeace pointed out to Stella Tyson. Well, it was hidden by trees. But it turns out it can be seen plainly in winter when the trees are bare.'

Thorne looked hard at his sergeant. Would he make the connection?

'I see,' said Ballantyne a little more positively. He frowned in thought for a moment and then said: 'Yes, that is – interesting.'

'Is it?' snapped Thorne. 'Why is it?'

Thorne could almost see Ballantyne's brain at work in the various expressions which succeeded each other on the sergeant's face.

'Well, let's see – it means Stella Tyson must have been lying when she told us about her trip to Wendover with Makepeace.'

Before joining the police Thorne had briefly considered a career as a schoolmaster. It was this side of him which now responded with a feeling of gratification. By proving himself a star pupil Ballantyne was demonstrating what a good teacher Thorne had been.

'Go on,' he said encouragingly.

Ballantyne, still concentrating, continued: 'But she was probably only lying about the date. They must have gone there for lunch but not when she said they did.'

'Explain.'

'Well, her story was too complex and detailed to have been invented on the spur of the moment.'

Thorne felt a distinct sense of pride. He was sure that Ballantyne would not have been capable of making this series of inferences without having been tutored by Thorne. Moreover no other sergeant who had ever been attached to Thorne would have risen to the challenge with such aplomb.

'Well done, sergeant,' he exclaimed.

Ballantyne nodded, still concentrating.

'Which means,' he continued, 'that Makepeace must have proposed to her at least a couple of months earlier, when the trees would have been bare.'

'Exactly,' Thorne agreed.

'But at the time he died, he was still with his wife – and that suggests he might have gone back on his proposal. So we get the possibility – ' At this point Ballantyne paused, frowning.

'Stay with it,' urged Thorne. 'Don't ever be frightened off by an implication.'

Looking a little appalled by the conclusion to which his own reasoning had led him, Ballantyne said wonderingly:

'We get the possibility that Stella Tyson is the murderer.'

'Motive?' asked Thorne.

Ballantyne shook his head faintly as if he didn't really believe what he was saying himself.

'Anger at being jilted,' he suggested. 'Oh, and there

could be a financial aspect. If their engagement was off, she might have been afraid he'd cut her out of his will and therefore she could have killed him to prevent it.'

'Excellent,' Thorne congratulated him. 'But don't get too puffed up. Right, we'd better pay a call on Mrs Makepeace.'

Ballantyne looked at him in surprise.

'You mean Miss Tyson, don't you, sir?'

'No,' said Thorne firmly. 'Why should I?'

Ballantyne was clearly baffled by the apparent reversal in the chain of reasoning.

'Well, to find out if she was lying,' he urged uncertainly.

'Ah,' said Thorne smiling. 'But we wouldn't, would we? She'd simply say that Makepeace told her about the folly, even though it was invisible when they were there. No, I think the trail leads us back to Mrs Makepeace.'

Less than twenty minutes later, the two policemen were at the door of the Makepeace cottage in Hampstead. Ballantyne rang the bell and very soon Mrs Makepeace opened the door. She greeted them both and then said:

'I'm afraid that after you phoned, a friend of mine called. She's here now.'

She led the way into her attractive, old-fashioned living room, where Thorne was astonished to see Stella Tyson seated at the dining table with documents and forms spread around her. Mrs Makepeace began to introduce them:

'Superintendent Thorne, this is – ' but then she shook her head in self-reproach. 'Oh, but I'm forgetting. You know Miss Tyson, don't you, superintendent?'

197

At this, Stella Tyson broke in ironically, 'Oh, they know me, Isobel. They think I'm a bad lot.'

Thorne nodded courteously at the former mistress of the dead man.

'Good morning, Miss Tyson,' he said, and then he turned to Mrs Makepeace, 'We had hoped for a private word with you, madam.'

'It's alright,' Stella Tyson intervened once more. 'I should get down to the market in any case.'

As Thorne had learned some time ago, Stella Tyson supplemented her earnings as an actress by selling jewellery and small bibelots in a central London street market.

Mrs Makepeace looked annoyed.

'Oh, but you mustn't, Stella – '

'I'll come back later, Isobel,' Stella Tyson reassured her. 'I'll just set up and then get my neighbour to look after the stall. These two have probably come to pump you about me in any case.'

'I most certainly hope not,' averred Mrs Makepeace. And then to Miss Tyson. 'Oh, Stella, could you bring a bottle of milk – no, better make it two – when you come back?'

'Yes, of course,' said Stella.

There was an uneasy silence while Stella Tyson made ready to go and then left. Then Mrs Makepeace, composed but, Thorne perceived, a trifle embarrassed for all that, explained to Thorne:

'You may have been surprised to find Miss Tyson here, superintendent? Well, the fact is, we're business partners now.'

'Really?' asked Thorne, who, in fact, was most surprised to hear of this slightly bizarre development.

'You probably think it's strange, wife and mistress going into partnership, especially after what I said

198

about Stella when you first interviewed me. But you see I didn't know her then. Oddly enough we liked each other at once.'

'How did you meet, madam?' asked Thorne quickly.

'Oh, it became necessary – arrangements over the will. Stella was very short of money and I agreed to release some of her inheritance at once.'

'And you became friends?'

'Well, yes, I suppose we did. The fact is, superintendent, we do have a bond. We're both lonely women.'

'May I inquire what business you're going into?' asked Thorne.

Mrs Makepeace pointed to the papers scattered on the table.

'We're just doing the preliminary paperwork, you see. I've registered it under the name of "Dorinda". It will be very like my old firm but under a different name. You know, cosmetics and fashion. Anyway, what did you want to see me about, superintendent?'

'When we first interviewed you,' said Thorne seriously, 'You told me that your husband had finished with Stella Tyson. Do you mind telling me on what grounds you said that?'

'Not at all,' said Mrs Makepeace, apparently quite cheerfully. 'Charles told me himself. You see he always kept me informed about the relationship.'

'I see,' said Thorne. 'Did he say why he was ending it?'

At this a decided air of doubt became apparent in Mrs Makepeace's manner and she bit her lower lip in indecision. But she rallied and said firmly:

'Yes, he did. He told me he'd caught Stella in bed with a young actor. He said that he'd always suspected she was a slut and now he knew she was.'

Thorne raised his eyebrows a trifle at this uncompromising assertion. Mrs Makepeace was far too perceptive not to register the implied criticism. She smiled grimly.

'I'm telling you what Charles said, superintendent. It's not at all what I think. I don't blame Stella in the least for having had a younger friend – '

'Lover,' interposed Thorne quickly.

Mrs Makepeace frowned and said sharply:

'Alright, lover. What's wrong with lovers? I only wish I'd had a few more.'

Thorne ignored this admission.

'Did Mr Makepeace know the actor by any chance?' he asked.

Mrs Makepeace shook her head.

'No. But he mentioned that he'd been touring with Stella in a comedy called – oh, it had "champagne" in the title – that's all I can remember.'

'And when was this?'

'Well, let's see,' said Mrs Makepeace, 'you're talking about when Charles broke with Stella?'

Thorne nodded.

'As I recall, it was shortly before we went for a long weekend to Wiltshire. That would make it – well – about the first week in June.'

Thorne nodded appreciatively and said:

'Thank you, madam, you've been most helpful.'

He rose to his feet and Ballantyne followed suit. Thorne began to turn towards the door but almost immediately turned back having, apparently, remembered something significant.

'Just one more thing, madam,' he said. 'Had Mr Makepeace given up drink?'

Isobel Makepeace looked surprised at this question.

'Good lord, no,' she said firmly.

'But,' said Thorne, 'his doctor had given him a strong warning about drinking too much.'

Mrs Makepeace smiled a trifle grimly.

'Oh, Dr O'Malley did that every year. Charles paid no attention.'

'I see,' said Thorne. Then he resumed. 'The warning was given on the 12th of April. So you actually saw your husband take a drink after that date, did you?'

'Oh yes,' asserted Mrs Makepeace confidently. 'I – '

But then she hesitated.

'Well actually no,' she admitted. 'You see the thing is Charles always pretended to give up drinking after one of O'Malley's death threats. So for a few weeks he'd confine himself to secret drinking. But he can't have given it up, can he? Or he wouldn't have drunk the poison in the whisky flask?'

Thorne nodded as if this were a point he hadn't properly considered before.

'True,' he said. 'Still it does seem possible that he might have cut down a bit.'

Mrs Makepeace shook her head.

'Oh, I doubt that very much, superintendent.'

Thorne smiled.

'Thank you, madam,' he said courteously.

The two policemen left the cottage and made their way to their parked car. As they were humming down the hill from the heights of Hampstead back towards the city, Ballantyne asked curiously: 'Why did you ask about the booze?'

Thorne smiled.

'Why do you think, sergeant?'

Ballantyne sounded a little uncertain when he replied: 'Well, I suppose you were wondering why he hadn't poisoned himself sooner than he did. But isn't it because he only kept the flask for emergencies, sir?

I mean, he had plenty of other booze at home and at his office.'

'Right,' agreed Thorne.

'What about this actor?' asked Ballantyne. 'The one she said Stella Tyson had been having an affair with?'

'I'm going to leave that to you, sergeant,' said Thorne. 'Find him, would you, and see what he has to say? Don't let on you know anything, even that he's supposed to have had it away with the actress. Just routine investigations, alright?'

'Alright, sir.'

Thorne glanced at his watch.

'Any chance of speeding up to a crawl?' he asked irritably, gazing vengefully at the traffic which now hemmed them in on the Chalk Farm Road. 'I'd like to get in a word with John Field before he leaves for lunch.'

But when they finally reached the Carr Sillmann office, they found that John Field had just left to visit a client in the country and would not be back that day. They drove back to Wood Street. Then Thorne despatched Ballantyne to seek out Stella Tyson's actor friend – and Thorne himself spent the afternoon in profound communion with his computer.

23

Thorne was drinking coffee and reading *The Times* while a Philippino girl called Solina was removing his breakfast things from the table. Solina had black eyes and a square jaw. She looked menacing until she smiled, whereupon she looked like an angel. As Solina approached the room door with her burden Milly dashed in wearing a riding habit with one boot missing. For this reason she moved in a strange kind of half-hop which looked extremely precarious and which nearly resulted in her crashing into Solina. But the new live-in servant was nimble and side-stepped just in time.

'Solina!' wailed Milly. 'Have you seen my other boot?'

The Philippino girl put down her burden on a side table near the door and crossed to the small sofa on the far side of the breakfast room. She pulled it forward a little and from behind it she unexpectedly pulled a riding boot. She held this out to Milly with her transforming smile. Milly smiled back and they looked like two angels enjoying a joke.

'Oh, you are a treasure,' Milly said fervently. She promptly sat down on the sofa and began tugging on the boot. Solina returned to the door, gathered up her dishes and departed for the kitchen.

'Lance, we've simply got to keep her,' said Milly when the girl was out of earshot.

Thorne, without looking up from his paper, murmured: 'Alright.'

Milly was so astonished she stopped struggling with her riding boot and gazed at him.

'What did you say?' she asked.

'I said "alright",' answered Thorne.

'No, you didn't,' said Milly vehemently. 'You said you didn't want a goddamn servant snooping around. You said you expected your wife to do the goddamn housework.'

'Really?' asked Thorne amiably, and this time he looked up from his paper. 'I thought I said "alright".'

Milly, who had finished tugging on her boot, stood up and approached him.

'Just now you said "alright",' she conceded. 'But you've been saying the other things for days.'

Then she looked at him suspiciously and asked: 'Hey, you're not starting to fancy Solina, are you?'

Thorne smiled. He didn't look quite as angelic as either Solina or Milly but he seemed benign enough to be admitted into their company.

'Enormously,' he said. 'But not as much as I fancy you. Come and sit on my lap.'

Milly, looking distinctly baffled, obeyed him. She put her arms around his neck. She kissed him on the tip of his nose.

'Lance,' she asked curiously. 'Why are you being so nice?'

'Because,' explained Thorne, 'I'm blessed with a nice nature.'

'No, you're not,' said Milly positively. 'I know. You're being nice because the case is going well. Isn't that it?'

'It's a factor,' conceded Thorne.

'Are you about to make an arrest?' asked Milly.

'Not quite,' said Thorne. 'But it shouldn't be too long now. Listen, Milly, I know you think I'm just a

204

detecting machine. But I love you. I didn't marry you for your money.'

'Hell, I know that,' exclaimed his wife. 'You hate my money.'

'No,' said Thorne analytically. 'I'm ambivalent about it.'

At that moment, the doorbell rang.

'God,' said Milly. 'That'll be the Thorntons.'

'Well, you want to ride, don't you?' asked Thorne.

'No,' said Milly. 'Not any more. I want to stay here with you.'

She threw her arms around his neck again and this time kissed him on the lips. Out of the corner of her eye she saw Solina appear once more in the doorway. The girl smiled politely when she saw how her employers were engaged.

'I know,' said Milly, freeing herself a little from the embrace. 'It's the Thorntons. Could you tell them I'll be along in a minute? No, make that two minutes.'

But she had hardly said these words when the telephone rang. Thorne reached out for it and, as he had expected, found himself connected to Ballantyne.

'Hello, sir,' the other greeted him. 'I'm in Paris.'

'Really?' asked Thorne. 'Naughty weekend?'

'On the trail of the actor. He's called Clive Wickham. He's in a show here on the Left Bank. I'm seeing him in an hour.'

'When will you be back?' asked Thorne.

'First plane I can get after seeing him. Shall we meet somewhere?'

'Well,' said Thorne, blowing a kiss to Milly who, reluctantly, was tip-toeing away for her riding appointment, 'I'm going over to Carr Sillmann to see Field. Then I wanted to see Stella Tyson but I'll have to get your report first. Tell you what, I'll go back to my office after seeing Field. Ring me there as soon as you touch down at Heathrow.'

'Right you are, sir,' agreed Ballantyne.

An hour later Thorne was in John Field's office. After greetings had been exchanged and Field had several times glanced meaningfully at the pile of papers on his desk as if to say 'don't keep me any longer than you have to', Thorne asked:

'When was the last time you saw Charles Makepeace take a drink?'

John Field smiled and then, to Thorne's mild surprise, answered with a poetic rhetorical question:

'When was the last time you saw a bird fly?'

'You mean,' said Thorne, deliberately lowering the tone of the conversation in the interests of precision, 'it was second nature to him?'

'Pretty much, yes.'

'By that do you mean he was drunk every day?'

'Well no,' admitted Field. 'In fact, like a lot of alcoholics, you could say he was never drunk. But he was always drinking.'

'Did you see him have a drink on the day of his death?'

Field thought for a moment and then said, 'No, I don't think I did.'

'The day before – ?' Thorne probed further.

'Well,' said John Field reflectively, 'I'm not absolutely certain – '

Thorne held up his hand.

'Alright,' he said. 'Try this. Think hard and tell me if it was more like a day, a week or a month since you last saw him actually take a drink?'

Field gazed at him blankly for a moment and then said: 'Look, superintendent, I was neither his brother nor his keeper. I didn't spend more time with him than I had to and so I don't actually remember seeing him take a drink. But he wasn't on the wagon. I know that.'

'How?' asked Thorne.

John shrugged.

'People would have noticed. It would have been talked about. Charles off the booze would have attracted as much attention as Sir Max on it. Besides – ' but he did not continue his line of thought.

Thorne pressed him.

'Go on,' he urged. 'It could be important.'

John Field sighed and resumed.

'Alright, I was going to say – if he'd been off the booze, he'd have seemed different. But he was just the same. Just as vicious.'

'Vicious?' asked Thorne, surprised by the adjective.

Field sighed again.

'Oh, I know. What's that Latin saying? Nothing about the dead unless it's something good. But whoever made that one up didn't know Charles Makepeace. He had the nastiest tongue of anyone I've ever known.'

'Really?' asked Thorne. 'And did he spread it about or were you the only one on the receiving end?'

'I got my share,' said Field bleakly. 'But it depended on his mood. When it was black, no-one was safe.'

'I see,' said Thorne. 'That's very interesting.'

'Is it?' asked Field. 'I'm glad of that.' He again glanced meaningfully at his piled desk. 'Well, if there's nothing else, superintendent – '

'I can see you're busy,' said Thorne, rising. 'Thank you for sparing me the time.'

And he left the office.

Thorne arrived back at Wood Street to find that Ballantyne had not yet returned from Paris. He decided

207

to have lunch in the staff canteen. He was half-way through his not very inspiring meal when Ballantyne turned up. The trip to Paris, it soon transpired, had been successful. The actor had provided confirmation of Mrs Makepeace's allegations.

'I think,' said Thorne. 'We have just about enough now.'

'For what, sir?' asked Ballantyne.

'To ask Stella Tyson why she lied to us.'

But when they confronted the lady she was, at first, completely defiant.

'I didn't lie,' she insisted.

'Not about everything,' agreed Thorne. 'But you did lie about one very important thing.'

'What was that?'

'That date,' said Thorne. 'I concede that everything happened as you described it. Charles Makepeace proposed to you in the lay-by above Wendover. But it didn't happen when you said it did. It happened quite a long time before.'

Stella sighed, and both Ballantyne and Thorne knew that the latter's theory was about to be vindicated.

'What makes you say that?' she asked finally.

'Because,' said Thorne, 'six weeks before his death, Charles Makepeace caught you in bed with another man. He was furious about it and he broke off the relationship there and then.'

'But,' protested Stella, 'That's simply not – '

Thorne quickly interrupted. He wanted to prevent her wading any further into lies.

'Sergeant Ballantyne has just returned from Paris where he interviewed an actor called Clive Wickham.'

Stella looked very glum at this news.

'Alright,' she said wearily. 'Bang to rights. It's true. Charley had a key to my flat. He walked in and caught

208

us. Super police work, superintendent. But does it really matter after all this time?'

'That's exactly what I'd like to know,' said the superintendent. 'In the first place, why did you lie to us?'

Stella smiled bitterly.

'I should have thought it was obvious. Charley broke off the engagement. I was deeply in debt. When you came and told me that he was dead I thought I might be able to get something from the estate. But only if I made out it was still on between us.'

'I see,' said Thorne. 'So while you pretended to be grief-stricken, you were really scheming to defraud the estate?'

'I wouldn't have put it quite like that!' said Stella bitterly. 'All I did was change the date a little.'

'I don't think it's as simple as that,' Thorne went on relentlessly. 'You were a beneficiary under Mr Makepeace's will. When he broke off his relationship with you, you were afraid he'd change that will. So you took steps to make sure he couldn't.'

Stella gazed at him in apparent incomprehension.

'Steps?' she asked finally. 'What kind of steps?'

And then a look of disgust and contempt appeared on her face.

'Are you suggesting that I killed Charley? To get his money? Is that the way your foul mind works?'

'Did you kill him?' asked Thorne simply.

Stella slumped back in her seat. She laughed, a small, bitter laugh.

'Oh, I had it away with other men once in a while. But the fact is I'd much rather have had Charley than any amount of money.'

Ballantyne had been watching Thorne's dramatic and relentless pursuit with admiration. But then to his astonishment he saw Thorne rise to his feet and, with no more than a curt nod, say:

'I see, Miss Tyson. Well, thank you very much for your cooperation.'

Ballantyne was so surprised that he failed to take his cue from his chief.

'Come along, sergeant,' Thorne prompted brusquely. 'Duty calls.'

But once they were in the car, Ballantyne exploded:

'I do not understand, sir. Why did you let Stella Tyson off the hook?'

'Hook?' asked Thorne mildly.

'All you had to do,' Ballantyne went on, 'was to press a little harder and she'd have cracked.'

'Like a rotten egg?' suggested Thorne with an unmistakable hint of mockery in his voice.

Ballantyne retorted angrily, 'Don't patronize me, sir!'

This seemed to anger Thorne. He snapped back, 'Then don't be so damned thick!'

At this, Ballantyne, who had never before shown much tendency to be insubordinate, said tightly:

'You know you can be a bloody arrogant – '

Thorne cut him off quickly.

'Just shut up, sergeant – before you say something you regret! Alright then, who do you think killed Charles Makepeace?'

Ballantyne snorted.

'Stella Tyson, of course.'

Thorne made a faint sceptical sound.

'Didn't she?' persisted Ballantyne.

'No, of course she didn't,' Thorne returned.

'How can you be so bloody sure?'

'Because I'm a bloody good cop.'

There was something in his manner which brought

Ballantyne down to earth. After a while he asked cautiously:

'Then who did kill him?'

Thorne shrugged.

'I've got no proof. But I know alright.'

'In that case, sir,' suggested Ballantyne with laboured politeness, 'would you mind sharing the knowledge with me?'

'Yes,' said Thorne quickly. 'I would mind. Get there on your own. You won't always have leading strings, sergeant. You'll have to catch the killers on your own one day.'

'I concede that,' said Ballantyne grimly. 'But if you'll forgive me saying so – '

But again Thorne cut him off irritably: 'And don't get pompous on me. Look, I *could* tell you my suspicions and my reasons for them, but for the time being you're more use to me checking my bearings. But I'll tell you this much, sergeant. We're getting damned near the end of the trail.'

24

'Why,' asked Ballantyne, 'are we going to see Tucker again, sir?'

'To clear up one or two points,' answered Thorne brusquely.

'Do you want to tell me what they are?' asked Ballantyne.

'Not specially,' replied Thorne. 'Like I said yesterday, I want you to get there on your own. Incidentally, you did make the appointment with Tucker, didn't you?'

'Yes, sir,' confirmed Ballantyne, 'he'll be expecting us.'

But when they reached Tucker's small laboratory in the East End of London, a white-coated technician led them to a glass-panelled door and, pointing, explained:

'He's in there.'

The two policemen looked through the panel and saw a room full of elaborate electronic and chemical equipment. It was not very large but the apparatus was clearly state-of-the-art. Inside the chamber were two men wearing elaborate gas masks, one of them clearly an observer and the other a technician.

'That's him,' said their guide, pointing at the observer. 'After you phoned, we had an urgent call from ICI to run a test for them. It'll only take a quarter of an hour. Hope you don't mind waiting. I could get you some coffee.'

'Looks fascinating,' said Thorne.

'It is,' said the other with a smile. 'You put three

drops of the substance you're examining in a crucible and ten minutes later you get about a hundred print-outs. Would you like to go in?'

'Why not?' asked Thorne. 'Would we need gas-masks?'

'Better safe than sorry,' said the technician. 'Over here in this cupboard.'

Two minutes later the two policemen joined Tucker and the other man in the sealed lab. For a while nothing much happened and then suddenly computer printers started chattering. A little later the man they took to be Colin Tucker, although they could not tell for sure because of the gas mask, beckoned them towards the door.

Once outside, the man removed his gas-mask and demonstrated that he was indeed Colin Tucker. Thorne and Ballantyne removed their masks too.

'Sorry about that,' apologized Tucker. 'But that series uses platinum and costs a fair whack to run. Otherwise I'd have abandoned it when you arrived. You were quicker than I thought you'd be.'

'Wouldn't have missed it,' said Thorne. 'What were you looking for?'

'The reactive sodium compounds,' Tucker explained. 'Sometimes we get a little pure chlorine. That's why the gas-masks. Come this way, gentlemen.'

He led them into his small office and bade them sit down.

'Now,' he said, looking from one to the other. 'What can I do for you?'

Thorne said:

'I believe you're a personal friend of Mrs Makepeace, sir?'

Tucker nodded and said: 'That's quite right, superintendent.'

'Would you call yourself an old family friend?'

'Certainly.'

'So you've had an opportunity to observe the Make-peaces' married life?'

At this Colin Tucker looked uncertainly from one to the other.

'I don't quite see – ' he began.

'I'll be frank with you, sir,' Thorne said. 'So far we've been basing our investigation on the assumption that there was a break-in at the Makepeace home and that the intruder put poison into Mr Makepeace's whisky flask.'

At this point Thorne glanced at Ballantyne. The sergeant was looking a trifle surprised but not too dismayed.

'But the fact is,' Thorne resumed, 'we have only Mrs Makepeace's word that such a break-in ever occurred.'

He glanced at Ballantyne again and this time he saw a look of dissent clear on the other's countenance. Indeed Ballantyne could not restrain himself from comment.

'But, sir – '

Thorne quickly silenced him.

'Not now, sergeant.' And then he turned to Tucker again. 'Did you ever observe any hostility by Mrs Makepeace towards her husband?'

It was Tucker's turn to look distressed.

'Well – I mean, they had their ups and downs. Everyone does but – ' then he shook his head unhappily and on a plaintive note, asked:

'Superintendent, what's going on?'

With uncharacteristic aggression, Thorne leaned towards him and almost snarled: 'A murder investigation, sir. That's what's going on. Someone murdered your old friend, Charles Makepeace, and I want to know who it was.'

Tucker was clearly dismayed.

'Well naturally, but – '

'I'm glad you agree, sir,' said Thorne pointedly. 'So would you mind if I offer you a piece of advice? Don't try to shield anyone. Do you understand, Mr Tucker? Tell me everything you know.'

'But I – '

'No, you don't need to say anything at this moment. I don't expect it. But think it over, Mr Tucker. And if you decide that you know anything at all that could help me in my investigation then please get in touch.' He turned to Ballantyne. 'Right, we'll be off then, sergeant. Unless there's something you want to ask Mr Tucker?'

Ballantyne, taken off guard, was reduced to shaking his head limply and stammering:

'No, not just at present, thank you, sir – '

But once the two officers were in the car, and Thorne was driving, Ballantyne gave way to the indignation that Thorne had known he was feeling.

'In my opinion, sir,' said Ballantyne reproachfully, 'that was sheer intimidation.'

Thorne sighed.

'The point is, sergeant, you can't do everything by the book. You have to be – a bit creative, sometimes.'

'By that, sir,' said Ballantyne with uncharacteristic sarcasm, 'I take it you mean lying to a witness?'

'What do you mean, lying?'

'You told Tucker we had only Mrs Makepeace's word for the break-in. But we have the old lady's word as well.'

'No,' said Thorne carefully. 'The old lady didn't actually see anyone in the act of breaking in.'

'That's just a damned quibble,' said Ballantyne indignantly. 'After all, she saw him climb the wall and – '

'Hang on, sergeant. Did you say "him"? The old lady said "her".'

'Alright, she wasn't clear about gender. But she saw someone go over the wall. You implied to Tucker that there was no independent evidence. Just what the hell are you trying on, sir? I mean do you really think Isobel Makepeace poisoned her husband?'

'What do you think, sergeant?'

'I think, sir – I think it would be nice to work for a governor who plays by the rules.'

'The rules sometimes wreck the game. Look, I'm not a bent copper but if we play this one too strictly the murderer will go free and you won't get any promotion.'

'The hell with – '

At this point Thorne swerved the car into the curb and pulled up so sharply that Ballantyne glanced round in alarm.

'What is it, sir?' he asked.

'What is it?' repeated Thorne. 'It's "The Medici", the best seafood restaurant in the City. Would you consider it an adequate bribe to stop your nagging if I bought you a lobster for lunch?'

There was no reply from Ballantyne but, as he opened his door to get out, Thorne glanced over at his junior and was relieved to see that Ballantyne seemed to be trying hard to suppress a smile.

25

'What should I wear, Milly?' called Thorne.

There was no answer. Clad in his vest and under-pants, Thorne walked to the door of the en-suite bathroom and opened it. Milly, who was wearing nothing whatsoever, was at the side of the bath with one foot up on its side. She was trimming her toenails with a pair of dainty scissors. Thorne admired the lithe curves of her girlish form for a while and then asked again:

'Milly? What should I wear?'

She looked round.

'Anything, Lance. Jeans, if you want.'

He gazed at her in surprise.

'But he's a baron, isn't he?'

'Something like that,' agreed Milly. 'But Jim's very laid back – not stuffy. We'll probably find everyone sitting around smoking pot.'

'Well, they won't sit around for long,' said Thorne. 'Because I'll arrest them.'

'Oh, no, I didn't mean that,' Milly hastily backpedalled. 'They wouldn't do anything to embarrass you.'

'Jolly decent of them,' said Thorne parodying an upper-class accent.

'What I really meant,' Milly tried again. 'Is that Jim's an easy guy to weekend with. No ceremony. No formality. Just a lot of laughs.'

'Well, that solves the dress problem,' said Thorne. 'I'll wear my cap and bells.'

He turned to go back into the bedroom.

'Incidentally,' said Milly. 'I've had a letter from Perugia.'

Thorne paused. 'Who's Perugia?' he asked.

Milly giggled.

'No, it's where, Lance. It's a town in Italy where my friends are staying. You know the Caplands, the ones with the Greek Island. They want to know if we're going there this summer. Because if we're not they've had lots of requests for it.'

'When would it be?' asked Thorne.

'Any time in September or October,' said Milly. 'All we have to do is tell them which fortnight and they'll reserve it. We could have it for a whole month if we wanted.'

'Alright,' said Thorne, 'I'll let you know soon.'

'But, Lance – '

'Now don't hassle me, Milly. I just can't make long-term decisions until the Makepeace case is wrapped up.'

'But I thought it was wrapped up?' said Milly plaintively.

'Not quite. But if this thing works – it's more like showbiz than police work but it could wrap up the case in a day or two.'

'Good,' said Milly. 'Then I'd be able to write later in the week.'

She reached up and switched on the needle shower.

The next morning, Thorne and Ballantyne went once again to the Makepeace cottage in Hampstead. But this time Thorne behaved quite differently. Instead of treating Isobel Makepeace courteously he leaned on her quite hard. Moreover he did so in the presence of Stella Tyson. First he gave Mrs Makepeace a slanted account of the investigation thus far. He omitted certain facts and overstressed others. He made it sound, although he did not actually say as much, as though the most likely solution was that Mrs Makepeace had lied about the break-in. The clear implication of this was that she was the guilty party although Thorne did not actually accuse her of being the murderer. Throughout, Thorne watched Ballantyne's reactions and was pleased to find that his sergeant was apparently not too dismayed this time.

But Stella Tyson did not accept Thorne's questioning. Indeed she became quite heated.

'How dare you talk to Isobel like this?' she snapped at one point.

Mrs Makepeace reached over and patted Stella on the arm.

'It's alright, Stella,' she said. 'But I must say I find it a trifle ironic. For some time I've been thinking that you were the chief suspect. It seems that I am.'

'It's crazy,' snapped Stella. 'Absolutely crazy.'

'Oh, I don't know,' said Isobel Makepeace soothingly. 'Not from their point of view. After all they've found out about Max and me. Of course that was all over years ago. But now Colin seems to have told them that I hated Charles.'

'Not exactly, madam,' Thorne intruded. 'But he has described being present at a number of heated domestic disagreements between you and your husband.'

'You're bluffing,' said Stella Tyson contemptuously to Thorne. 'You haven't got any evidence against Isobel. You can't have.'

'Perhaps she's in the best position to judge that,' suggested Thorne icily. Then he rose and Ballantyne rose with him. As they departed, Thorne said quietly to Mrs Makepeace:

'You have my number if there's anything you want to tell me.'

In the car, when they were on their way back to Wood Street, Ballantyne said: 'I think I see what you're up to, sir. But isn't it dangerous?'

Thorne sighed.

'Probably. But have you got a better idea? We'll never get proof of guilt. The best we can hope for is a confession.'

'Perhaps,' agreed Ballantyne, but then added. 'But couldn't it misfire in some way?'

'Nothing ventured,' said Thorne mournfully. 'It's a tricky one, I admit. Look, can you hang around over the weekend? I've got to go to the country. But I have an idea it might break.'

'I'll put in a little overtime,' said Ballantyne cooperatively, 'if you don't tell the union. You know, sir, I still don't quite see how you got there.'

'Wait till it's all wrapped up,' said Thorne, 'and I'll draw you a map.'

It worked exactly as Thorne had planned. Except that it went a bit beyond what he'd planned.

On the Friday evening, Thorne and Milly were driving out to spend the weekend on a small estate belonging to one of Milly's titled friends. Ballantyne, as a result of Thorne's request, was working late. He had plenty of admin to keep him busy and planned to leave his office at about seven-thirty or eight. It began at about quarter to seven. His phone rang, and when he answered it he heard an obviously distressed Stella Tyson at the other end. He could also hear, in the background, the bustling noise and laughter of the street market in which she worked. It seemed, as he later discovered, that on Friday evenings it stayed open until seven-thirty.

Stella told Ballantyne that she was afraid that Colin Tucker might be considering suicide. When he asked her why she thought this, she said it was a bit complicated. It was only when it was all over that Thorne and Ballantyne put together the sequence of events.

They went like this: after the visit of the two detectives to the Makepeace cottage that afternoon, Stella Tyson had determined to do something to help her new friend and partner, Isobel Makepeace. She had, as Thorne had intended that she should, concluded that the police had decided that Isobel was the guilty party. It seemed to Stella, again as Thorne had planned, that the police were basing their thinking chiefly on the evidence of Colin Tucker. Stella decided that she owed it to Isobel to have a word with Tucker.

However, Stella was by no means certain that Isobel would agree to the plan. She decided, therefore, that it must be done in secret. Reluctantly, but with firm resolve, she found an opportunity to copy Tucker's number from Isobel's address book. Then, when she left the cottage later to go to the street market, she called Tucker from the first available phone box.

It proved to be a frustrating call. First she got through to a secretary. Then she was inadvertently disconnected. Then, on redialling, she got a wrong number. Finally she got back to the secretary and after another frustrating wait at last found herself talking to Colin Tucker.

'Yes?' he asked.

'We've never met, Mr Tucker,' said Stella earnestly, 'but I felt I had no choice but to ring you. The police have just been round to interview Isobel Makepeace. I was with her. The thing is they think she killed Charley.'

There was a moment's pause before Tucker said softly:

'Charley?'

'Sorry,' said Stella. 'I meant Charles – Charles Make-peace. Superintendent Thorne's got the idea Isobel poisoned him.'

'But that's inconceivable,' said Tucker hotly. 'Anyone who knows Isobel – she couldn't – I mean, she could never – '

'Of course not,' agreed Stella. 'But innocent people do sometimes wind up in prison. You see, unbelievable things can happen, Mr Tucker, and especially when people like you make accusations.'

'But you can't think – I would never – I do assure you – '

'All I know is that Thorne thinks that you believe that Isobel killed Charley.'

'He can't do. At least – '

And then there was a pause, so long that Stella began to think she'd been disconnected once again. But finally Tucker spoke again. And this time his voice sounded weary and resigned.

'Don't worry, Miss Tyson,' he urged. 'Isobel won't be arrested. I promise you that.'

'How can you?' asked Stella Tyson.

'I'll get in touch with Thorne. Yes, I'll – I'll write him a note.'

'Phone him. That's the way. Give him a ring on Monday. Look, Mr Tucker, I know that Charley was your best friend but – hello? Hello, are you there?'

Stella discovered that once again the line had been disconnected. She began to redial but then stopped. Would it be wise? After all she had begun to get Tucker to act responsibly. If she called him back she wanted to have a tape recorder so that she would be able to record his denial that he had accused Isobel. She hung up and left the phone box.

For the rest of the afternoon and evening, however,

the conversation with Tucker nagged at Stella's thoughts. It wasn't that she doubted that he had meant what he'd said. It was something about the way that he had said it which troubled her. But she couldn't put her finger on precisely what it was that she found disturbing.

It was during a chat with Daffs, who was the neighbouring stallholder and a friend, that she suddenly perceived what was wrong. Stella and Daffs were similar in some ways. Daffs was also a "resting" actress who dabbled in jewellery and bibelots. But Daffs was a good twenty years older than Stella and not nearly so worldly or well-educated.

Daffs was in the middle of telling Stella a story about an uncle of hers who kept a cat's home in the country when she became aware that she had lost her audience.

'What's up, Stell?' she asked, a trifle reproachfully. 'Gone off into a brown study?'

Stella looked at Daffs' large and reassuring face.

'Something's wrong, Daffs,' she said.

'What, you mean the skinheads?' asked Daffs in her slight Cockney accent. The market had recently been plagued by a group of rowdy youths.

'No, not the skinheads,' said Stella impatiently. 'Daffs, do you know how to play word associations?'

Daffs gazed at her without comprehension.

'It goes like this,' said Stella, 'I say a word and you tell me what it suggests to you – alright? Now "note". What does the word "note" suggest?'

Daffs screwed up her face and thought. While thinking she automatically reached forward and replaced an enamel box on its shelf after a potential customer had deposited it negligently in the wrong place.

She finally suggested:

'Music?'

Stella was about to shake her head when Daffs herself added an alternative.

'Suicide?'

Stella looked at her hard for a moment and then jumped to her feet.

'Look after the stall, Daffs,' she ordered. 'I have to make a phone call.'

And it was then that she phoned Ballantyne.

26

Thorne was not happy about leaving London. As the Jaguar sped along the M25 towards Canterbury he reproached himself with moral cowardice. He should have told Milly that this weekend could prove a critical one for his investigation and that he really had to stay in London. He had, in fact, been on the point of doing so several times as they prepared to leave. The trouble was that it was quite a big occasion for Milly. The lady of the estate where they were spending the weekend was one of her oldest friends and one whom she had not seen for years. Even then Thorne might have cried off had he not been aware that in recent weeks he had given Milly quite a hard time. On several occasions when she had organized an expedition or outing of some kind, pressure of work had prevented him from accompanying her. Thorne tended sometimes to regard Milly a little the way the sailor in Coleridge's 'Ancient Mariner' thought of the albatross – as a burden that kept him from doing the things he should be doing. But whenever the possibility of actually losing her crossed his mind he realized that she wasn't a burden at all but a companion who provided most of what was joyous in his life. Thorne appreciated Milly's money and the things it could buy. But he also feared it as an acid that might corrode his resolve and his ambition. But his ambivalent attitude towards her wealth meant that he never had to ask himself if it was her money that bound him to her. It was Milly herself with her exasperating, enchanting ways.

'Slow down, Milly,' said Thorne. 'You're doing eighty.'

'That's not much,' returned his wife.

She was right. It wasn't. It was, in fact, about the speed of the traffic stream in the central lane. Cars in the fast lane were slipping smoothly past at over a hundred miles an hour.

Thorne realized that he had not asked her to slow down because she was exceeding the legal limit but because he felt an urgent need not to get too far from London. But, of course, that was foolish. They were heading for an estate near Canterbury and there was nothing to be gained by delaying tactics.

'Milly,' he said, trying to sound stern. 'I'm a cop. It would be embarrassing to be nabbed for speeding.'

'But I'm driving,' she retorted.

'That,' said Thorne ironically, 'would not diminish the embarrassment.'

Milly sighed, but she slowed down and, at the first opportunity, she edged into the slow lane.

It was about ten minutes later, when Milly started telling Thorne about a programme she had watched on television the night before, that the car phone bleeped. Thorne had no doubts who it was. He picked up the instrument and asked, 'Ballantyne?'

Then he listened for quite a long time, occasionally prompting or questioning but, for the most part, absorbing what his sergeant had to say. Milly was not at all happy at this development, suspecting that it constituted a threat to her weekend. She realized that the worst had happened when Thorne concluded the conversation:

'Right. Get over there. I'll join you as quickly as I can – what? About ten miles east of Greenwich I'd estimate.'

In the forlorn hope of staving off the inevitable Milly immediately said: 'Lance, I hope this doesn't mean – '

But he cut her off brusquely.

'Sorry, darling. No option. Get off the motorway at the next exit. Then I'll drive.'

Milly made no further protest.

As soon as they came to an exit, she left the motorway and at the top of the departure ramp she and Thorne changed places. Thorne thereupon took them back down but on to the other side of the motorway. A little earlier he had reproached Milly with doing 80. Now he had the Jaguar up to 120 in about two minutes. It took them just half an hour to reach Tucker's small lab in the East End.

As they neared the low concrete structure they saw that the door was open and a uniformed constable was on guard. Outside an ambulance was parked at the curb. Behind the ambulance was a marked police car with a uniformed constable at the wheel and also a car which Thorne recognized as the one Ballantyne was currently using. Across the road, a knot of local people, mostly children, had collected and was watching the events.

'Wait here,' said Thorne briefly to Milly.

He left the car and approached the uniformed constable. He flashed his warrant card. The constable nodded and said:

'They're bringing him down now, sir.'

Thorne entered the building and crossed the small entrance hall to the staircase. He started up it but soon stopped. From the floor above a small procession had started down: two stretcher bearers carrying someone whom Thorne could not, because of the angle, see but whom he knew must be Tucker. They were followed by Ballantyne and a uniformed sergeant.

Thorne stepped down again out of their way. When they reached ground level he saw that Tucker was apparently conscious. His eyes were open although his face was contorted with pain. He groaned faintly. As soon as Ballantyne had drawn abreast, Thorne asked him:

'Do we know what he took?'

Ballantyne shook his head.

'No idea, sir. He left a note but he never finished it or signed it. It doesn't say what the poison was. He was unconscious when we found him, so perhaps he intended to name it. He came to a bit when we started moving him.'

'Right,' said Thorne. 'I'll question him in the ambulance. You'd better meet me at the hospital.'

Thorne followed the stretcher bearers out of the building. There was a faint stir amongst the spectators on the opposite side of the road when the mournful little procession appeared. The children stopped playing and gaped.

Thorne waited at the rear of the ambulance for the bearers to deposit Tucker inside. Then he entered the vehicle and crouched beside the self-poisoned man. The driver looked at him questioningly but nodded when Thorne flashed his warrant card.

Thorne noted that Tucker's complexion seemed perfectly alright. His skin did not, like that of other poison victims Thorne had professionally encountered, have a blue, or white or even yellow tinge. But his features were periodically contorted by spasms of pain. His eyes were closed. Thorne felt the ambulance jog slightly as someone else entered it. Thorne glanced round and then said disapprovingly:

'Milly, what do you think – '

But his wife held up her hand.

'I'm coming, Lance,' she said firmly. 'I've been part of this case. I think I've earned the right to see it through.'

There was some truth in what she said. It was against regulations for Milly to be present but Thorne didn't feel specially official at that moment. He nodded and turned his attention back to Tucker. Milly sat down on the lowered bunk opposite.

The steps were raised and the door of the ambulance was slammed. A moment later the vehicle's engine came to life and soon the ambulance rolled smoothly away from the curb and gathered speed.

Thorne waited as long as possible. He didn't want to harrass the desperately afflicted man but he had to get all the information he could from him while he was still able to give it. Finally he reached down and shook him slightly:

'Mr Tucker,' he said, 'Mr Tucker can you hear me?'

Tucker opened his eyes, and gazed at Thorne with what, for a second, almost seemed like friendly interest. The little, grey-haired man had a pleasant face, Thorne noticed for the first time. He looked like a schoolteacher or rather like an actor playing a schoolteacher in a sentimental television serial.

Apparently free from pain, for the time being, Tucker smiled and said:

'It was true, you know, superintendent. Charles really was my best friend.'

'I believe you,' said Thorne. 'But first off, Mr Tucker, what have you taken?'

Tucker, still smiling, shook his head.

'No way,' he said faintly. 'Not taking any chances. No antidote in any case. According to my calculations should be dead by now. One thing didn't anticipate – the pain. Never expected it would be so painful.'

'I'm sorry,' said Thorne, feeling almost hypocritical at the inadequacy of the conventional phrase. He hurried on: 'Mr Tucker, Charles Makepeace – he wanted his money back – was that it?'

Tucker nodded.

'Yes, that was it. Part of it. He was entitled to his money, of course. But paying it back would have ruined me just then. I asked him to wait. No, the truth is, I begged him to wait.'

'And he wouldn't?' asked Thorne.

Tucker murmured, 'My best friend – but – well, the fact is, he could be – '

The little man shook his head faintly as if the challenge of finding, or perhaps employing, the right word was more than he could face.

'Vicious?' suggested Thorne.

For a moment Tucker gazed at him expressionlessly. Then he nodded.

'That's it,' he said sadly. 'It wasn't just the money. He called me a derelict – seedy little failure – me, his best friend. So when he went to the loo I just reached out for the first phial on my shelf and poured it into his flask.'

'How did you get hold of it?' asked Thorne. 'The flask?'

'He'd been drinking from it. It was just sitting there on my desk where he'd left it.'

'You assumed he'd come back from the loo and drink it?'

Tucker shook his head as energetically as he could manage.

'No. Didn't assume. It was a gesture. Not real murder attempt. Another minute and I'd have poured it out again. Sure of that. But he came back, picked up flask, screwed on top and put it in his pocket. I watched in – in amazement at what I'd done.'

Tucker's face suddenly contorted with pain. Almost like a child, he gasped:

'Oh, it does hurt.'

Thorne said nothing and, in a moment, the spasm having passed, Tucker resumed: 'The next few weeks were hell – simple hell. I picked up the phone a dozen times to warn him but couldn't find the courage. After all, it would look like a cold-blooded murder attempt. I couldn't face them knowing – him, my family, newspapers. Then, as the weeks passed, I began to feel that I was going to get away with it.'

'I think I understand,' said Thorne. 'You thought he'd probably washed out his flask. Is that it?'

Tucker nodded slightly.

'Yes. But I think I also began to doubt that it had ever happened – it didn't seem to tally with anything I knew about myself. And then I made the – terrible discovery. Learned that Charles was off the booze. Knew then he was carrying it around – a kind of time bomb – '

At this point Tucker gave a gasp, that turned into a groan, of pain. It seemed to signify a spasm more intense than any thus far. He raised his hands a little and Thorne immediately seized them and gripped them as hard as he could in the attempt to supply some degree of counter-irritant. As he did so his position changed slightly and he found himself face to face with Milly. She smiled a little and nodded encouragement.

27

'The breakthrough came,' said Thorne, 'when I found out that Miss Tyson had got her dates muddled.'

But Isobel Makepeace interrupted: 'No, superintendent, not muddled. Stella lied about them. We tell each other the truth.'

Thorne nodded. He was glad to be spared the necessity for euphemisms.

It was the following Monday. He and Ballantyne were in the Makepeace cottage by appointment. It seemed only fair to give the two women in Charles Makepeace's life a debriefing on the circumstances of his death.

'When I discovered that the trip to Wendover had been months earlier,' Thorne continued, 'then everything fell into place.'

Isobel frowned as if she still hadn't quite grasped the complexities of the story.

'So Colin put the poison into Charles's flask in a moment of desperation. Is that right?'

Thorne nodded.

'And then naturally,' she went on, 'he was surprised that Charles stayed alive. But what happened next?'

'I think I know, Isobel,' said Stella Tyson. 'Colin Tucker slowly became convinced that his – well his impulsive murder attempt had gone wrong. He probably thought that Charley had washed out his flask or perhaps had given a number of people a sip from it and they'd all got tummy aches and nothing worse.'

Thorne said approvingly.

'That's precisely how it was, Miss Tyson. Tucker began to think Makepeace, and that meant himself as well, was safe. But then, about a week before Mr Makepeace's death, Tucker learned that Mr Makepeace was on the wagon. He realized that the flask was probably still full of poison.'

'And so that,' said Isobel slowly, 'is what induced him to break in here. Mrs Wagstaff opposite thought it was a woman. Colin is very slight like a woman.'

'Yes,' said Thorne. 'It's a grim irony that if you and your husband had dined out as you'd originally planned, Tucker would have found the flask and emptied out the poison. It was sheer bad luck that you came home before he'd found it.'

Isobel Makepeace nodded.

'So the point is that we all assumed that the intruder had put the poison into the flask and he'd really been trying to take it out.'

'Precisely,' said Thorne. 'It was when I'd got that far that it became obvious that Tucker must be the chief suspect. It gave him a motive. At the date of the break-in he'd have harmed himself if he'd harmed Mr Makepeace but two months earlier he had his back to the wall, financially speaking.'

Isobel Makepeace sighed deeply. Then she took up the tea-pot and began topping up the tea in their cups.

'Poor Colin,' she murmured.

Stella looked at her with, for the first time, resentment.

'Isobel,' she said reproachfully.

But Isobel shook her head.

'Oh, Colin's not an evil man, Stella. He must have had a ghastly two months. And as for Charles, well the autopsy proved that he wouldn't have lived long with his heart.'

She turned to Thorne again.

'Will Colin ever wake up, superintendent?' she asked.

Thorne shrugged very slightly.

'The doctors can't be sure. He apparently used an organic poison which they haven't been able to identify. At first it was all they could do to keep him alive in intensive care. Now he's stable but in a deep coma. It's quite likely that he'll stay that way.'

'I shall get in touch with Dora,' said Isobel to Stella Tyson: 'his wife. We'll have her to dinner, shall we?'

Stella Tyson smiled faintly.

'If you like,' she said.

As the two detectives walked towards their car, Ballantyne said:

'I think you hit the right note, sir.'

Thorne, as if faintly startled by the implication that he might have done otherwise, said sharply:

'What?'

'Well – sympathetic but detached.'

'Oh – ' said Thorne but clearly his mind was on other things.

Ballantyne asked:

'After you'd found out about the folly, how long did it take you to figure the rest out?'

'Three to four minutes,' said Thorne promptly.

Ballantyne said ruefully:

'And I never got there at all.'

'That,' said Thorne 'may be because you never side-stepped. Lateral thinking can be a copper's friend. You got stuck with thinking the break-in was when the poison was put into the flask. So did I until I found out about the folly.'

'What about instinct, sir?' asked Ballantyne.

'Invaluable,' said Thorne.

'Any way to speed up acquiring some?'

Thorne smiled.

'Healthy living. What are you doing this weekend?'

'Going to the ballet,' said Ballantyne. 'With Nurse Fletcher. She's down for the weekend. She's from the hospital.'

'I remember her,' said Thorne. 'Small, brown hair, brown eyes.'

Ballantyne grinned.

'Hazel, actually, her eyes. But I didn't know you'd noticed her, sir.'

'Saw her when she took your pulse. You both seemed to enjoy the process. Still, a date with Nurse Fletcher may be bliss but it's not healthy living. A jog round the park and bed by eight is what I had in mind.'

'Is that what you're doing, sir?' asked Ballantyne mischievously.

'No,' he admitted. 'We're going shooting and feasting on a lord's estate. But then I've already got my copper's instinct. Tell you what, pull up at the "White Hart". You can buy me a couple of drinks and we'll do a quick analysis of the case.'

28

Ahead of the dog, which had been nosing purposefully through the Yorkshire heather, a grouse suddenly took wing. It whirred up from the purple heath but it did not get far. There was the report of a shotgun and the bird, struck in mid-flight, tumbled to earth, a limp bundle of feathers. The dog, instead of retrieving, rushed excitedly away in the opposite direction barking as if to celebrate. It was a young, ill-trained dog. Eyeing it reproachfully, Thorne strode to the fallen bird, picked it up and stuffed it carelessly into an already bulging game pouch.

'That's five in a row,' said Milly when he had returned to her. She was smartly dressed for the field but had no gun. 'Don't you ever miss?'

'Yes,' said Lance, 'but not very often.'

He looked at the sky. Clouds were beginning to converge upon the sun.

'Shall we go on?' he asked. 'We're likely to get wet if we do.'

'I don't mind,' said Milly. 'They're bringing out a picnic – champagne and stuff – later.'

'I'd just as soon go back to the car and try that pub in the village,' said Thorne.

He sounded gruff. Milly asked: 'What's the matter, Lance? What's eating you?'

'Nothing,' insisted Thorne, but not very convincingly.

It was more than a week since their grim ride in the

ambulance together, and Thorne had been edgy ever since.

'It's still the Makepeace case, isn't it?' asked Milly.

'I just don't like unhappy endings,' said Thorne with a slight laugh.

Milly took his arm. The dog frolicked around them.

'Look at it this way, Lance,' Milly suggested, 'if Tucker wasn't in a coma, he'd be facing a murder trial.'

'Exactly,' said Thorne.

'Well then,' said Milly. 'He's better off in a coma.'

'But that's not the point, is it?' said Thorne grimly.

'Then what is?' asked Milly in surprise.

Thorne sighed and did not answer at once. Then he said: 'My career. Tucker's no use to me in a coma.'

It took Milly a moment or two to get his meaning.

'No use – ' she repeated in a baffled tone. Then the naked meaning of his words reached her and she snorted in disgust. 'Oh, I see. You want him on trial. You want the goddamn publicity.'

'Well, why not?' returned Thorne. 'I've worked damned hard on this case. What's the point in catching killers if you don't get the credit? Hell, Milly, I thought you understood me by now.'

He turned and looked her straight in the eye. She shook her head sadly, wondering if she'd ever understand the full force of his ambition. But before she could find appropriate words to express her feelings, the dog, which had been circling and nosing, started another grouse. At the first hint of its rising whirr, Thorne, almost by instinct, whipped up his gun, swung round and fired. But the shot proved too difficult even for him.

'Damn!' he exclaimed angrily, as he watched the small, red-beaked bird flap desperately away across the heather.